Title: Saratoga secret

Lexile: 710
Reading Lvl: 7.7

SARATOGA SECRET

SARATOGA SECRET
BETSY STERMAN

DIAL

BOOKS

FOR

YOUNG

READERS

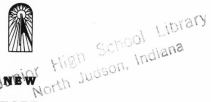

NEW

YORK

Published by Dial Books for Young Readers
A member of Penguin Putnam Inc.
375 Hudson Street
New York, New York 10014

Designed by Julie Rauer
Printed in the U.S.A. on acid-free paper
First Edition
1 3 5 7 9 10 8 6 4 2

Library of Congress Cataloging in Publication Data
Sterman, Betsy.
Saratoga secret/ Betsy Sterman.
p. cm.
Summary: In 1777, as General Burgoyne and his British troops
invade the upper Hudson River valley, sixteen-year-old Amity
must carry a secret message to the Continental Army
to give warning of an impending attack.
ISBN 0-8037-2332-6
1. New York (State)—History—Revolution, 1775–1783—Juvenile fiction.
[1. New York (State)—History—Revolution, 1775–1783—Fiction.
2. United States—History—Revolution, 1775–1783—Fiction.] I. Title.
PZ7.S83815Sar 1998 [Fic]—dc21 97-49678 CIP AC

FOR SAM, WITH LOVE

AND IN LOVING MEMORY OF ROB

SARATOGA SECRET

CHAPTER
1

❖

Amity stepped out into the dawn and shivered. Though it was June, a chill lay over the hilltop farm. She called to Ned, but he was already loping toward her out of the shadow of the woodpile.

"Good Ned," she said as she stroked the dog. "Come along, Lady's waiting to be milked."

The cowshed was less than fifty paces from the house, but even hurrying that short distance made her uneasy. The woods beyond the pasture were dark. Trees nearby cast shadows that might hide an enemy. She kept Ned close beside her, though he knew better than to dash to the cowshed and startle the animals. He did not need her grasp on him, but she needed his warmth. More than that, she admitted, she needed him to make her feel safe. For this summer something else chilled the air.

Fear.

It was a strange new feeling to Amity. It had never been her nature to be afraid. Oh, long ago, when Schoolmaster Jowdy would gather the children together at harvest feasts and tell scaretales of ghosts and bogles, she and the others would clutch each other in mock terror, their screams mixed with giggles. But that had been different. Lately turned sixteen, she had felt herself beyond fearful imaginings. Yet since the beginning of summer, when the crops were but ankle high in the fields, she had heard the fear in people's voices and seen it in their faces. Now it seemed to drift like a cold mist over the farms of the upper Hudson River valley.

An invasion is coming, people said. An enemy army is headed down from Canada, straight toward *us*! Thousands of redcoats—with muskets and bayonets and cannons!

"Is it true?" Amity had asked her father.

She had been glad to see him shake his head. "It's only talk," he answered. "An ugly rumor."

"But . . ."

"Amity, the war is a faraway thing," he said. "The fighting is nowhere close to us, nor likely to be so."

She knew that General Washington's battles and skirmishes with the British army were taking place hundreds of miles to the south, in Pennsylvania and New Jersey. Everyone knew it. But this summer everyone was afraid.

"All this invasion talk is nonsense," Father had told her. "Think, Amity—war is fought on battlefields, not on rocky hills and river bluffs."

"But someone said—"

"Someone with as much sense as a pudding!" Father had said with a sweep of his arm. "Armies need roads to march on. The British are not such fools as to send men and cannon through forests."

Solid, clear-headed Father. As always, his words made sense, but talk of the invasion would not go away.

Amity lifted the latch on the cowshed door and hurried inside. Jess, the old plowhorse, looked up from chewing a twist of straw, and Lady lowed softly. For a moment Amity stood still, glad for the warmth and familiar animal smells. Later, when the animals were in the pasture, she'd shovel out the manure, barrow it to the heap behind the cowshed, and spread fresh straw. It was a task she and Simon had done together, but now . . .

She shook herself. Thoughts of her dead brother were never far away, but now there were no tears, only a deep aching sadness. She patted Jess, smiled at the still-sleepy sheep, and put the milking stool down next to Lady. Ned settled beside her in a thin wisp of sun that had crept through the open door.

She talked quietly to Lady as her fingers coaxed the warm milk into the bucket. Talk was a comfort, even though there were only the animals to hear. She missed the sound of Simon's voice. If he were here now, he'd be talking to her, sharing his thoughts as if she were his friend rather than his older sister. There had been only two years between them, and they had been as close in spirit as Polly and Matt Thomas, the twins who lived on the farm across the road.

Oh, Simon, I miss you.

She fancied she heard Polly's scolding voice. "Amity Spencer, you think too much. Why do you fill your head with so many ramblings?"

Amity never had an answer to that. For years she had wished

to be more like Polly—full of liveliness and chatter, never giving in to wonderings and dark thoughts. But it was not her way, and now that Simon was gone . . .

There she was, thinking of him again.

Suddenly Ned scrambled up and Amity felt a jolt of fear. "Ned! What is it?"

But he had dashed out of the cowshed. Her heart thudded in her chest until, over his barking, she heard the rattle of a wagon and the clinking of metal.

"Cheppa John!" she cried.

She ran to meet the peddler's wagon as it came into view on the hillpath. Tin pots and pewter jugs swung from its high wooden sides, jangling as they glinted in the pale morning sun. His visit was a surprise, as always. Trading took him up and down the valley for miles, and downriver too, from the port town of Stillwater to Albany, a city of churches and schools and fancy houses, she had heard. Oh, to be a peddler and see those places!

Cheppa John halted the wagon and jumped down from the high wooden seat. He flung her a smile as he strode to the well to draw a bucket of water for his horse.

"I'm so glad to see you!" Amity exclaimed. She stroked Toby and was startled to feel the horse's sweat.

"You've pushed Toby hard," she said.

"Aye," he said. "I had reason to hurry."

Amity drew in her breath. She waited for him to say more, but he was silent and she could read nothing in his face. He had a way of looking directly at a person as if to search out one's true thoughts, but he could veil his own thoughts behind his eyes.

"What reason?" she asked.

"There is word of the war," he said. "And . . . there is this."

From the folds of his tunic he drew a small book. It was hardly larger than his palm, and printed on coarse paper. He tilted his hand so she could read the title.

"*The Tale of Robin Hood.* Oh, Cheppa John!"

She wanted to throw her arms around him in thanks, but it would not do. She would have done so with his father, old John the Chapman, for he had been almost as dear to her as her own father. All through her childhood he had peddled in the valley, carrying messages and healing people's ills as well as selling and bartering goods. To Amity's and Simon's delight, among the pots and cloth and butter churns in his wagon were chapbooks, small books of poems and tales printed in faraway Boston or New York Town or even London.

Young John—Cheppa John, he had early named himself— had grown up in the trade. He was twenty now, and his father dead of the pox three years past. Now *he* was the one valley folk depended on for their goods and medicines and news.

And books.

She was used to his bringing books for barter. Sometimes, after she and Simon had pored over a book until they knew it by heart, he would take it back in exchange for another. But there was something different this time. She saw it in the way he looked at her, the way he grasped her hand to place the book in it. She felt a jolt of surprise when he covered the book with his other hand and wrapped his fingers around her own. It was as if he were giving her something more than the book.

She looked up at him quickly and felt her face redden. To cover her confusion she said, "I'll ask Mother what we may barter for it."

He shook his head. "The book is a gift," he said.

"A gift? But why?"

"Because you have turned sixteen," he said with a smile.

"But I don't underst—"

"Hush." He withdrew his hand and laid one finger across her lips. She felt it move slowly up to brush her cheek. Then he curled the finger into his fist as if locking in the feel of her face.

She searched his eyes. "Cheppa John, I . . . I thank you for the book, but . . ."

The door of the house opened. "It's you, peddler!" Will Spencer called. "I thought I heard your wagon. Welcome."

Beside him, holding three-month-old baby Jonathan, stood Amity's mother, Joanna Spencer. She looked at Cheppa John questioningly. "Is there news?" she asked.

Cheppa John turned to them. "Aye," he said.

"Then come in quickly. Amity, finish your chores."

Cheppa John gave Amity a quick glance, then strode toward the house. Amity stood still, hugging the book to her. "Oh, Cheppa John," she whispered inside her head, "I do thank you."

She wasn't sure her thank-you was for the book alone. Whatever he had meant by his strange behavior, somehow he had put a seal on her growing up. Her birthday had gone unnoticed by her parents, and no one seemed to have paid any mind to her passing out of childhood.

No one except, perhaps, Matt Thomas. Everyone expected her to marry him one day, and she supposed she expected that too. Their farms were near each other, their families were friends, and ofttimes Polly teasingly called her "Matt's other twin."

"Some day we'll be true sisters!" Polly liked to say.

Matt himself had said nothing, but lately she had felt his eyes on her in a new and different way. The way Cheppa John had looked at her.

She was startled out of her thoughts by Ned. He pushed against her, herding her toward the cowshed.

"Yes, yes, Ned, you're right. We must finish." She slid the book into her apron pocket and hurried back to the animals. Hastily she drove the sheep out of the shed and signaled Ned to herd them into the pasture along with Lady and Jess. She shooed the hens into their coop and tossed grain at them, drew the morning's water from the well, and hurried to the house, a rope-handled bucket in each hand. In her haste, water and milk sloshed onto her skirts.

She looked down at the wet stains, frowning. Now Cheppa John would see her all of a mess. Yet there was nothing for it.

Hurry, she told herself. He has news of the war. Now maybe we'll hear at last that the invasion was only talk.

She knew the minute she stepped inside that something was wrong. Her father's pleasant face had darkened into a scowl. Her mother stood at the plank table, her hands kneading bread dough and one foot rocking the cradle, but her face had gone white. Both of them were staring at Cheppa John.

"Near eight thousand men," he was saying. "Grenadiers and artillerymen as well as Regulars. German hirelings, with their own commanders. Horses and supply wagons by the hundreds, and dozens of cannon. The king has spared nothing."

"So it's true," her father said slowly. "I can scarce believe it."

The ropes slid out of Amity's hands and the buckets thumped down on the floor. She stared at Cheppa John, feeling the pleasure of his visit and his gift wither away.

"This is not to be believed," Will Spencer said, slowly shaking his head. "There's no way to bring an army down from Canada— no road to march troops on, nothing but wilderness."

"Aye, nothing but trees and rocks and marshlands," Cheppa John agreed, "and swarms of blackflies enough to drive men mad. Yet they're dragging cannon and supply wagons where you'd think only deer could go."

The baby whimpered and Amity saw that her mother's cradle foot had stopped as if frozen. Amity reached over and began the rocking again. No one spoke.

"Strangest of all," Cheppa John went on at last, "is the general who leads this army. Gentleman Johnny Burgoyne he's called, because even on this campaign through wilderness he sleeps on silk sheets and eats off silver plates. A fine dandy he is, but also a fine general. Word has it that the invasion was his idea. He plans to capture the whole river valley for the king."

"Impossible!" Will Spencer exploded. "I tell you, he'll get no farther than Ticonderoga. Fort Ti is strong enough to stop any army."

He turned to his wife with a reassuring smile. "We have no need to worry, my dear. Before long this fancy general will be turning back to Canada, wishing he'd never left England."

Joanna Spencer did not smile back. Her eyes were on Cheppa John. "Can Fort Ti hold against this Burgoyne?" she asked.

The peddler shrugged. "We have strong defenses there," he said. "Men, artillery . . ."

Amity thought it not a real answer.

Her father jabbed an iron poker at the hearthfire. "An invasion through deepwood—why, it's madness!" he muttered into the flames. Then he turned with a short laugh. "And it will fail," he said. "Silk sheets and silver plates cannot take Fort Ti."

Even so, when he left the house a few minutes later for his morning work in the fields, Amity saw him take his gun and shot pouch with him.

She walked outside with Cheppa John and stood holding Toby's harness as the peddler climbed up onto the wagon.

How like his father he is, she thought. He even looks like old John the Chapman—the same sharp planes in his face, the same slate gray eyes, and the same long hair pulled back in a club.

His hair was dark, though, not gray. And his clothes fit his tall frame better. Just like his father's, they were, and just as strange—buckskin breeches and fringed tunic belted with a

1 1

braid of deerskin, a finely tucked white linen shirt under the tunic, and a black three-cornered hat.

Once, when she had been a child, she had asked John the Chapman why he wore such odd clothes. He had taken her on his lap and solemnly explained.

"You see, Mistress Amity, it's because I'm half Indian, half French, and half Yankee," he had said, and she, being too young to have mastered her sums, had asked if he had any more "halfs" in him.

How he had laughed! But young Cheppa John, on the edge of his teens, had looked at her as if she had said something very wise. Now Cheppa John was a grown man, and different from Matt and the other farm boys she knew. It was not just that he wore buckskin and they wore homespun. They were open-faced and plainspoken, talking of trap lines and turnip crops, and clenching their fists when they cursed King George and the war. Cheppa John talked of places and people far beyond the valley farms. He spoke of ideas too, as Father did. And there was something more. Often Amity saw in his gray eyes thoughts he would not share. Perhaps, she thought, he has more "halfs" than he allows folks to see.

Now, watching him take up Toby's reins, she peered up at him. Whatever had passed between them an hour before was gone. His mind seemed turned only to the invasion.

"Is Father right?" she asked. "Will Fort Ti hold?"

Again he shrugged. Then he pulled himself out of his thoughts and looked down at her, as if to tell her something important. But the moment passed.

"Farewell, Amity," he said.

Without another glance he flicked the reins over Toby's back and steered the wagon down the hillpath to the road below.

CHAPTER

2

❖

The ragged man came two days later. Amity, working at the woodpile with her father, saw him stumble out of the woods at the edge of the pasture. He lurched toward the house, swinging the butt of a musket at Ned, who had leaped up at him, snarling and barking. Will Spencer dropped his ax and snatched up his gun.

"Call off the dog!" the man shouted. "I want only food! For pity's sake, food!"

Later, at the table close to the hearthfire, the man gulped cornmeal mush and slabs of cold bacon. Amity peered at him curiously. He was gaunt and hollow-eyed, his clothes in tatters and his boots torn.

He sat back finally. "Many thanks, ma'am," he said to Amity's mother. "First food I've had in days, unless you count raw rabbit."

"Where have you come from?" Will Spencer asked.

"The northern woodlands," he said. "Left my farm two steps ahead of the invasion."

Amity heard her mother draw a sharp breath.

Her father's face tightened. "Did you see Burgoyne's army?"

"Aye, saw 'em, heard 'em, smelled 'em. Watched 'em work their way through the woods like crows through a cornfield." The man tore off a large chunk of bread and pushed it into his mouth.

"We heard there were cannon," Will Spencer said, "though I can scarce see how . . ."

"Aye, cannon," the man said. "And wagonloads of shot enough to blow the sun out of the sky."

He leaned forward and spoke urgently. "You folks ought to be pulling out of here. Burgoyne's men will dig up your crops and butcher your animals and burn your house to the ground just like they did mine."

Amity felt herself shiver. The man's words and his haunted face put ice down her spine.

"How far are they from Fort Ti?" Will Spencer asked.

"Can't say, but they're coming on fast," the man answered with a shake of his head. "That Burgoyne's the very devil, the way he drives his men. I say pack up and go while you can."

At last the man sat back from the table and looked slowly around. "I had me a place like this," he said. "Main room, with a hearth as big as yours. Sleeping room just like the one over there—aye, and a loft above. A lot of space for a man alone, but I figured to take me a wife some day, raise up some young ones. But Burgoyne put paid to all of that. Everything's gone."

Amity stared at him. The lines and hollows in his face had made him seem older than Father, but now she saw that he was not much older than Cheppa John.

Joanna Spencer set another piece of gingerbread before him, but he shook his head. "I'll take it along, if you don't mind," he said. "And some of that cheese and bacon, if you can spare it. Don't know when I'll get another meal."

They saw him to the top of the hillpath, a bundle of food slung over his shoulder. He gave the small farm the same long look he had given the inside of the house.

"Don't count on the redcoats passing you by up here on this hill," he said. "Pack up and go, else you'll see them make ruin of everything you have."

With a small wave of farewell he went down the hillpath. They watched until the curve of trees hid him.

Will Spencer turned to his wife and daughter. "Take heart," he told them. "Fort Ti will hold." Then he walked to where he had flung down the ax, and went back to splitting wood.

Amity followed her mother into the house. "What if Burgoyne does get past the fort?" she asked, but Joanna Spencer did not answer. She lifted the sleeping baby from the cradle and held him close.

The day wore on like any other, filled with ordinary tasks, but there was a difference. Will Spencer and his wife had withdrawn into a silence that rang in Amity's ears. She longed to run down the hillpath to the Thomas farm across the road. There she would find talk and maybe even laughter, for Polly and Matt and their rosy, cheerful mother were not ones to let the threat of redcoats push them into a brooding hush.

If only Mother were like Mistress Thomas, she thought. It

was not the first time she had made this wish, and as always she felt a rush of shame.

Joanna Spencer was a thin, quiet woman. She had been pretty once, Amity remembered, with smooth, pink skin and thick honey-colored hair under her white mobcap. But since Simon's death it was as if a light inside her had flickered out.

It was only a year since Simon had died—strong, lively Simon, at thirteen already growing into a tall, well-muscled lad who could split logs and heft fence rails almost as well as his father. He had taken to farming from the time he could toddle about tossing grain to the hens.

Simon—a son to pass the farm to some day, as Will Spencer had received it from his father.

Amity felt the old sadness pull at her. How odd that she, always small and thin like her mother, had been able to fight off the throat-stabbing fever and get well, while strong, sturdy Simon was the one whose life had been choked out of him.

Not a word had her mother said about Simon after they had buried him in the small graveyard near the house. Two other graves were there, smaller ones. Those little brothers were dim in Amity's mind, for they had died when scarcely older than baby Jonathan. It was Simon who had been so real. Just into his teen years, he'd been more than her brother. He'd been her friend.

Like Polly—no, different, for Simon was solid and dependable like Father, with none of Polly's flightiness. You could share things with Simon that you'd never tell Polly. And since Polly was impatient with books, it was Simon who shared each new chapbook the peddler brought.

As she carried a load of wood into the house, Amity found the whole morning darkened by the ache for Simon and the fear brought by the ragged man.

The ragged man's words hung over the midday meal. She longed for talk, for answers to questions, but she found no way to intrude on her parents' heavy silence.

At last Father looked up. "Jess has burrs in his coat again," he said in a flat voice.

"I'll brush him," Amity said eagerly, and hurried to clean the pewter plates and cups. She ran out to the pasture where Jess grazed near Lady and the sheep.

She always found comfort in the quiet horse. Today, as she attacked the burrs with a stiff straw brush, she told him her worry about the ragged man's warnings. "What should we do, Jess?" she said. "Father says Fort Ti will hold, but what if . . . ?"

She had always put her what-if's to Simon, but now there was no Simon to talk to. There was no way to talk *about* him either, except with Jess. Say Simon's name and a curtain would drop over Mother's face. She would turn swiftly to her tasks, her lips pressed tight as she punched her fists into the bread dough or sent the wooden shuttle clattering through the loom.

Father didn't talk about Simon either. Sometimes, as Amity worked beside him, she knew he was thinking of the son who had been growing into such a strong helper, and she worked harder, faster, fighting for a word of praise.

I'm strong too, she longed to cry out. Haven't you seen how I do Simon's tasks as well as my own?

Now, as she picked the last burrs from Jess's coat, she pushed aside such thoughts. Better to imagine the talk at the Thomas farm across the road. Maybe, after chores were done, there would be time for a visit. This day she needed to be with the high-spirited Thomases more than ever.

"There now, Jess," she said. "Mind you stay away from those prickle bushes till Father and I get them pulled up." She gave the horse a pat and went back to her chores in the silent house.

At last it was late afternoon. She had churned the morning milk into butter and set the round butter pats in the cooling cellar. Scrubbed the churn clean. Helped Mother wash and hang up Jonathan's baby-linen. Filled the water crock again.

Now . . . now! She was free until eventide milking.

She ran down the hillpath to the Thomas farm and there, as she had expected, talk of the enemy invasion was peppered with laughter.

"Look, Amity," Polly cried, "I'm practicing my curtsies for the fancy general in charge of the king's army. Come help me!"

She grabbed Amity's hand and held tight, trying to balance on one foot until she tumbled them both over in a laughing heap.

"Fancy the king sending a dandy to frighten us," said plump Mistress Thomas. "And he's brought along wagonloads of handsome uniforms and French wine! Think of it!"

"Won't that be a treat for our men at Fort Ti!" said Matt, heaving a pair of fresh-skinned rabbits onto the table. "What a celebration they'll have!"

"Oh, how I'd like to be one of them and celebrate too!" Polly cried. She grabbed up a rush broom and perched it on her shoulder as she marched about the room, her bright red hair bouncing under her mobcap.

Polly's antics filled the room with laughter. There was even a smile from Isaac Thomas, Polly and Matt's father, who sat by the fire, sick again with a cough.

"I'm off to join the Continentals!" Polly cried. "Come, Amity—let's both go after Gentleman Johnny Burgoyne!"

"Fine lot of help a pair of girls would be," Matt teased. "It takes men to fight the king's army—men like me!"

Mistress Thomas gave him a fond smile. "Fancy the king's army running from a boy of sixteen years," she said. "You'd best leave the fighting to the real soldiers at Fort Ti."

Matt's face, so like Polly's, went serious. "I could be as much a soldier as any of Gentleman Johnny's bloodybacks," he said. "Sixteen's not too young to fight. Or to think about marrying." He threw a quick glance at Amity.

Amity felt her face redden. She didn't know how to act when he said such things.

Polly would not have turned away in confusion. Polly had been born with womanish ways. Last March, at sugaring off, Amity had watched her laughing up at Ben Tyler, her eyes dancing at him, even though everyone knew Ben meant to marry Charity Bates as soon as spring planting was done.

"Never you mind," Polly had whispered afterward. "It's not Ben Tyler I'd want to marry anyway. It's . . . no, I can't say his name. It's a secret."

"A secret? Why?" Amity had asked.

"Because . . . oh, I'll tell you anyway, it's no fun keeping it to myself. The only fun of having a secret is in the telling. It's one of Dorf the miller's sons."

"Which one?" Amity had asked, and Polly had giggled.

"I haven't decided yet, but it scarce matters. Oh, Amity, what fun to be wife to a man whose work is grinding nice clean grain instead of forever mucking up after cows and sheep and pigs! Just think of it!"

Amity thought of it. Maybe Polly wasn't meant to be a farm-wife.

Maybe I'm not either, she thought now, daring a glance at Matt. Married to him, I would spend my life as I spend it now—milking, feeding chickens, churning butter. Carding wool, spinning, weaving. Stitching bits of cloth together into quilts. Waiting for the one big excitement—the visit of the peddler.

A startling idea burst into her thoughts. What if I were wife to the peddler?

Wife to Cheppa John! She remembered his look as he had given her the book, felt again the feel of his finger on her cheek. Did she dare imagine he had such thoughts about her?

Amity pulled in her breath. What would it be like to join her life to his? To travel with him about the countryside? To visit Stillwater, maybe even go as far downriver as Albany? There would be new places to see, new people to meet, new talk to listen to. And new things to learn, for he'd teach her about healing herbs and balms just as he had learned them from his father.

Against the sound of Polly's chatter Amity let her fancy grow. She saw herself sitting high on the wagon seat beside Cheppa John, smiling her greetings to farm folk gathered in their doorways. She'd keep the wagon stock neat, not tumbled about as it often was. She'd have him build shelves for the cloth, and compartments for the ribbons and laces and fancy buttons.

And a special place for the chapbooks. As Cheppa John mended a farmwife's cooking pots or treated a child's rash, she would gather the other children around her and read tales or rhymes aloud to them. And afterward she and Cheppa John could trade the chapbook for a length of homespun or a crock of honey.

"Amity?" said Polly's voice. "Why, Amity, you look all muzzy-headed. And your face is so red! Whatever are you thinking about?"

Amity looked up at Polly. Never say a word of this to her, she warned herself. A secret is not something to tell. It is something to hug close and never speak of to anyone.

She shrugged off Polly's searching look, then faced Matt and turned the talk away from marrying. "My father says Burgoyne will not make it past Fort Ti," she said.

Matt laughed agreement. "Of course not," he said.

"Your father is right," Isaac Thomas said with a cough. "Never a single redcoat will we see in this valley."

A while later, her fears lifted, Amity climbed back up the hillpath with a light step. Once more the Thomases had worked their magic on her spirits.

Ned bounded down to meet her, and she ruffled his fur. "Pay no mind to what that ragged man told us this morning, Ned," she told him. "Never a single enemy soldier will come this way!"

CHAPTER

3

❖

For weeks afterward she managed to push the war to a far corner of her mind. There were no more strangers bursting out of the woods with scaretales of invasion, and only scornful talk about the British general with the odd nickname.

Father and Master Thomas are right, she told herself. By now Burgoyne has met defeat at Fort Ti. Our soldiers have turned him back to Canada with whatever is left of his army. He's lost his cannons, his wine, and all his wagons full of fancy uniforms—all left behind in a scramble to retreat. Likely our men at the fort are celebrating right now!

She pictured the soldiers throwing down their muskets and rushing out of the huge fort. She saw them ripping open the wagons, dressing themselves in pieces of abandoned finery. And the commander of the fort himself . . . was he parading about in one of Gentleman Johnny's curled and powdered wigs? What merriment Polly could make of that!

"Amity, you missed a row of carrots," her father's voice said. They had been weeding the vegetable field for hours, and he sounded as weary as she felt. She straightened up and frowned at the endless sea of vegetable tops. Beets, carrots, onions, potatoes.

What difference does it make? she wondered. What we will eat is under the ground, so why can't a few weeds have their space on top?

The July sun was high and hot, and she was out of sorts. Why hadn't Cheppa John come back with the news? She longed to see him again, to listen to him tell how the enemy had given up and fled. And to fit him farther into her new and secret dream.

A flash of light caught her eye—and another. Ned scrambled out of the shade of the woodpile and began barking. At the same instant she heard the familiar rattle and clink.

He had come at last!

She ran to greet him, but drew back as the wagon clanked to a stop. Polly would know what to say, but Amity felt her own mouth go dry. Now, with the new way she'd been thinking of him, she was almost afraid to meet his eyes. What if his gift had meant nothing after all? What if he had just been dallying, the way Polly had flirted with Ben Tyler?

She reached for Toby's harness. Stroking the horse, she managed to unlock her tongue. "It's good you're here, Toby. Last week's windstorm knocked apples from the trees, and I'll find some for you. You too, Cheppa John, if—"

Her father had come up behind her. "Hush, child," he said sharply. "What news, peddler?"

Child! The word stung. Didn't she figure in the marriage thoughts of Matt Thomas, and maybe even Cheppa John?

To call her "child"—and in front of him!

She bit back the hurt and forced herself to look up. It would

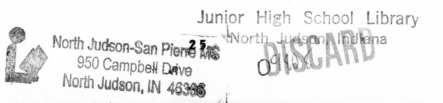

help to see the special smile Cheppa John had given her along with the book.

But he had only the briefest glance for her. He was looking over her head at her father.

"Fort Ti has fallen to Burgoyne," he said.

Amity moved closer to the hearthfire. Sun streamed in through the open shutters, but Cheppa John's news chilled the whole room.

"How could such a thing happen?" she heard her father ask.

Cheppa John threw himself onto the high-backed wooden settle near the hearth. Amity thought she had never seen him look so down-spirited.

"Burgoyne had his men drag cannon up the mountain overlooking the fort," he said.

"Up Mount Defiance?" Will Spencer said in astonishment. "Why, everyone knows that's too steep a climb for any but goats."

"Aye, so everyone always thought," Cheppa John said. "So our men never bothered to defend it. But Burgoyne is a clever strategist, and he has men to spare. He ordered artillerymen to force their way up, and by nightfall he had cannon pointing straight down at the fort, set to pound it to dust at first light."

Amity saw her father's fists clench. "Are you saying our men surrendered Fort Ti without a fight?"

"There . . . was no formal surrender," Cheppa John said. "At dayrise Burgoyne marched his troops into an empty fort."

Amity saw her parents exchange looks. "But our men!" her father said.

"Escaped under cover of the dark," Cheppa John said. "They left everything behind—cannon, ammunition, stores of food. Lucky to have taken their lives with them."

Silence lay on the room.

"It would have been madness to stay," Cheppa John said quietly. "Burgoyne had every advantage."

"Where is our army now?" Joanna Spencer asked at last. She wore a tight, closed look. Her hands, cutting meat for the stewpot, moved in fast, nervous motions.

Cheppa John made a wry face. "It's hardly an army anymore," he said. "Only men with axes and prybars. They're somewhere in the forest, retreating—chopping down trees day and night."

"But that's . . . that's clearing a way for Burgoyne!" Amity burst out.

"Nay, building barriers to stop him," Cheppa John answered. "Damming streams into bogs to swallow men and horses, making barricades of trees across every trail."

Will Spencer looked hopeful. "Then he can't be mounting a swift pursuit," he said.

"Aye, every mile is a torture," Cheppa John agreed. "His men are sick with flux and bitten raw by blackflies, but . . ." Amity saw the peddler's gray eyes narrow. "But they clear away the barriers near as fast as our men can make them. There's plenty of British muscle left. Sooner stop the wind than stop this army."

Only the crackle of the fire cut into the silence.

Cheppa John stood and walked to the table. He drew a map out of his tunic and laid it before them. "It's the river road Burgoyne is after," he said, pointing.

Amity looked at the line that ran beside the river, from Stillwater south to Albany. "Armies need roads to march on," Father had said.

So Burgoyne would have a road after all.

She shivered. The war was no faraway thing now. It was coming close to their very doorstep.

"Once he gets past Stillwater," Cheppa John went on, "he'll have an easy march to Albany."

"And find a warm welcome there, I warrant," Will Spencer said bitterly. "The town is filled with Tories."

Tories! Amity thought with a jolt. Men—women too—who were loyal to the king instead of to the newly united colonies. Everyone said that they spied and schemed and were almost as dangerous as enemy soldiers.

"Aye, Burgoyne will be handed Albany on a serving trencher," Cheppa John said.

"Does it matter so much?" Amity asked, then reddened. What if he thought her question witless?

He took it seriously. "The British already hold New York Town," he said. "With Burgoyne in Albany, all the Hudson River will be in enemy hands. The northern colonies . . . I mean states, will have no way to send men or money or supplies to General Washington."

His hand made a sharp slice through the air. "Our new United States of America will be cut in half."

"And the war as good as lost," Will Spencer said. Amity had never heard his voice hold so much despair.

"Aye," Cheppa John said. Slowly he rolled up the map.

Amity saw anger rise in her father's face. He stabbed the poker at the fire and sent up a shower of sparks. "There must be something we can do," he said. "We must take some kind of stand against Burgoyne."

"There's no standing up against an army this size," Cheppa John said. "Once he breaks clear of the wilderness, we'd best let him have Stillwater and get on to Albany as fast as possible. At the least it will put an end to the war."

"And an end to our independence!" Will Spencer raged. "I cannot go along with that! We must fight this man!"

Joanna Spencer's hands stopped cutting the meat. "No!" she cried. "Let him have the road he wants and leave us in peace!"

Her husband spun around. "Peace? What sort of peace will it be with redcoats swarming over our land? Do you think an army feeds itself only from its supply wagons? I say the man must be stopped before he reaches Stillwater."

Two spots of red burned in Mother's cheeks. "And who will stop him?" she blazed. "You? Young Matt Thomas, who's barely sixteen? His father, who's too sick to work a day in his own fields? Be sensible, husband! Even if all the valley men stood together, it would be farmers with fowling guns against cannon!"

Amity's breath caught in her throat. She had never seen her mother so afire, or heard her pour out such a stream of words.

Cheppa John stepped into the uncomfortable silence. "There's talk of General Washington sending some of his own men, though he can ill spare them. And the Stillwater militia might be joined by others from Massachusetts or Pennsylvania."

Father ran his hand over his chin in thought. "A pitiful small force," he said, "but better than nothing."

"No, it's the same as nothing," Mother said.

Only the snap and hiss of the fire made a reply.

At last Cheppa John stirred himself. "It may be all for the best," he said. "Some folks say this whole war is only a foolish row over a threepenny tax on tea."

Will Spencer made an angry gesture. "That's Tory talk," he flared. "It was the king who forced the war on *us*—setting that tax without our consent, filling Boston with troops . . ."

"Some folks say it is a king's right to do that," Cheppa John said.

Amity saw her father lean across the table and search Cheppa John's eyes. "And what do you say, peddler?" he asked slowly.

Cheppa John turned his face to the fire. He seemed to choose his words with great care. "I say I'm for independence, but now it matters little. Once Burgoyne crosses to this side of the river and gains the road to Albany, we'll all be English subjects again, like it or no."

Amity shifted uncomfortably in her chair. For the first time she found herself wishing there would be no more talk in this room.

Days later, when she visited the Thomases, she found no laughter, only the same argument.

"But think!" Matt cried. "If we don't stop Burgoyne, we'll lose the war!"

"Then so be it," Isaac Thomas said around a cough. "We'll go on with our lives as best we can. There is nothing to be done."

Matt thrust out his chest. "There *is* something," he said. "I heard Farmer Nash and the others talking at the mill. They said General Washington is sending an army of Continentals to Stillwater, with its own generals. They said more men are needed, and—"

"Grown men," his mother snapped. "Not farm boys."

"Anyone with a weapon will be welcome," Matt insisted. "Ben Tyler is going, and he's but a few years older than I am."

Mistress Thomas gave her bread dough an angry punch. "What do lads like you and Ben Tyler know about soldiering?" she cried.

"We'd learn quick enough," Matt said. "We'll be with the Stillwater militia, under the command of General Benedict Arnold, and he's fought many a fight against the British."

"Oh, Matt, I think you'll be a fine soldier!" Polly exclaimed as she ran to him. "Ma, don't you see? Pa's too sick to go, so Matt will take his place."

Amity's throat knotted. Her own father had no one to go in his place.

But surely he would not go off to fight Burgoyne and leave his family alone.

Would he?

CHAPTER

4

❖

As summer slid toward September, ordinary tasks turned urgent. Autumn's chores had to be done at summer's end, because Will Spencer was going to war.

"Hurry, Amity!" he would say. "Heft the other end of this fence rail."

"Make haste, child," her mother would call. "The sausages need to be stuffed."

Hurry . . . hasten . . . rush. Tear short, stubby carrots out of the ground, plunge half-grown cabbages into crocks of brine, drag baskets of small potatoes down to the root cellar.

"Scarce fit for eating," Joanna Spencer said through tight lips, "but we may need them." Tugging on a heavy basket, Amity hoped they would not have to eat such hard, knobby lumps.

Turnspitting was the worst task. For long hours she stood at the hearthside, turning the heavy iron rod over the fire, dodging grease that dripped and sputtered from haunches of venison. Her arms ached and her face felt scorched, and still her father shot more deer, skinned them, and slid the haunches onto the turnspit rod.

"Are there any deer left in the woods?" she asked once, trying to keep her voice as light as Polly's.

He had not answered.

Why must there be so much meat? she wondered as she wearily turned the spit. Bacon and venison nearly filled the root cellar, and more hung in the smoke chamber. Enough for a whole winter's eating, and more.

Why so much? she asked herself again. The answers made her breath stop.

Because Father expects to be gone a long time. Because he might not come back at all.

This was a truth that could not be pushed away. He could be killed warring against Burgoyne.

She wanted to spend every minute with him, and it was a relief when the turnspitting was over. Now, after inside chores, she flew out of the house to work with him. She helped him mend the leather-hinged shutters and fit a new latchbar to the pasture gate. She worked beside him stacking firewood until a wall of split lengths stood beside the house. She was glad now for her new strength.

More than ever before, though, she wished for Simon. He would be the one to listen and share the terrible fear she had to keep to herself: What if Father comes back from the fighting with dreadful wounds, Simon? What if he doesn't come back at all? Simon, what shall we do without dear, dear Father?

She heard her own voice clearly, but Simon did not speak back to her.

One day, while helping Father spread straw on the strangely bare vegetable field, her feelings rushed out. "Why must you go?" she cried.

He did not seem surprised at her outburst. He looked across the hills, now red and yellow with early autumn, then met her eyes.

"When your grandfather Spencer came from England," he said slowly, "he chose this bit of land because it put him in mind of the Yorkshire hills where he grew up farming for a wealthy lord. He gave me the privilege of growing up here on this farm, free of a master, and the land is as dear to me as it was to him."

"But then why leave it to go off and . . . and try to be a soldier?"

"Hush," he said gently. "The land is dear, Amity, but dearest to me in all the world are your mother and you and Jonathan. I cannot stand by and let the king take from those I love the very thing I have so much come to believe in."

"You mean . . . independence?" she asked.

He nodded. "It is the right way for a new country," he said. "A hard way, but right. I must do whatever I can to make sure that, having chosen it, we do not lose it."

"But why *you?*"

"Not I alone," he said. He put his arm around her shoulders and smiled down at her. "Do you remember how you once put a question to old John the Chapman about 'halfs'?"

She nodded, her face flushing. Why would he suddenly think of such long-ago childishness?

"You have learned your sums well since then," he said. "Think now about how every part of this war all adds together—your father and many other fathers, plus brothers and sons and nephews and men with no families at all, each free and independent and loyal to the new United States. Alone we are powerless against Burgoyne or any other enemy, but if we stand together we can turn our loyalty into might. Think, Amity. Loyalty is something the king can't force from sixpence-a-day redcoats or from farm boys bought like cattle from German princes."

He had always taught her and Simon to think, to question, to puzzle things out and search for their own answers. Now she wondered how men armed with little but loyalty could stand up to enemy cannons.

But she dared not ask. He was smiling at her again, and she knew he wanted her to take strength from his words. She forced herself to smile back, and they turned again to their work.

There was work in the evenings too. Amity and her mother put aside their spinning and weaving to help Father make lead-shot. Together they melted lead over the fire, poured it into bullet molds, and sorted the cooled shot—some for the gun he would take with him, some for the one he would leave behind.

He was leaving them behind too—a woman, a girl, and an infant. Most of the nearby valley women were already gone. Ben Tyler's new wife, Charity, had fled home to her parents west of the valley. Schoolmaster Jowdy's prim sister had gone with her, and Dorf the miller had sent his wife to faraway cousins.

We'll be the only ones left, Amity thought. We and the Thomases.

Mistress Thomas had early made up her mind not to leave.

"Let this fine General Burgoyne bring his redcoats up to my door," she said with a twitch of her plump shoulders. "We'll invite them in to tea, won't we, Polly? Aye, and feed them such a brew as will burn their bellies! Why, they'll likely lay down their weapons at our very feet!"

Amity had turned to Polly with a smile. "Oh, I'm so glad you're staying," she said, but Polly pouted.

What's wrong? Amity wondered. It was not likely that Polly was afraid to stay. There must be something else.

Mistress Thomas bustled on. "We have no family but my sister Kate in Stillwater," she said, "and that's no place to be, not with soldiers swarming all around."

"Soldiers would be better company than sheep," Polly muttered. "I wish we could go to Aunt Kate's."

So that was it. Amity understood, for she had wished to be in Stillwater too. It would be closer to the fighting, and dangerous, but closer also to Father. He and the other valley men would be in camp upriver from the town, and there might be ways for him to send letters to them. That would be a comfort, she told herself. So would being in the midst of townspeople.

That was the real comfort she wished for, she admitted. People to be with and talk to. Danger shared with others, not faced alone on a hilltop.

She had heard much of Stillwater, but had never seen the town. Mother, weak from childbearing or stillbirths, or burdened with a sick infant, had always needed her at home. Simon had been there once, riding in a neighbor's wagon with Father and their broken plowblade. When they had come back, Amity had flooded him with questions. "What is Stillwater like? Did you see the river? Did you go to the inn? Did you meet Polly's aunt Kate? What is she like?"

But Simon could talk only about the horses men were riding, the saddle he'd seen in the window of a saddlery shop, and how he'd watched while the blacksmith forged a new blade for the plow. Before long Amity's father had put an end to her questions.

"Leave him alone, child," he had said. "There's work to be done."

Amity remembered how her face had burned over that hated word. Her parents never used it for Simon, though she was the older one and Simon the younger. Was it because Simon was a man-to-be, and she was not?

What does it matter now? she asked herself sadly, and let Mistress Thomas's voice seep back into her thoughts.

"Polly and I are glad we'll have you and your dear mother nearby," Mistress Thomas was saying. "It will be hard for us without Matt, but it's always good to have close neighbors, isn't it, Polly?"

Polly, over her pout, nodded and squeezed Amity's hand.

"A pity you have no family to take you in—it's not easy to be alone with an infant," Mistress Thomas babbled on, "but you can depend on Polly and me for company. And when your dear father comes back from the fighting, won't he be glad to find you here instead of gone off to beg shelter from strangers."

Amity knew her mother had never had a thought of leaving

the farm. "Our place is here," she had said firmly to Father, with an unusual flush of color in her cheeks.

He would leave his hunting gun with them for protection. "All sorts of people may be about," he had said. "Deserters, foragers bent on stealing food. You must not let anyone leave you to starve."

Both Amity and her mother could handle the gun. Joanna Spencer had once brought down a deer that had leaped the pasture fence to graze, and after Simon died Father had made sure Amity knew how to load, aim, and fire. He had talked of taking her into the forest to hunt some day. But now the gun would not be for shooting animals.

It was Cheppa John who one day put the question. "Mistress Spencer, would you shoot a man?"

Joanna Spencer's chin had lifted. "Aye," she had said, "if he is an enemy."

Amity shuddered, and Cheppa John had turned to her.

"And you, Amity," he said. "You may find yourself doing things you never dreamed of. Are you so minded?"

His question startled her. What would there be to do other than each day's endless chores?

"What things?" she asked.

He turned aside from her question. "War puts many of us outside ourselves," he said, almost to himself. She had stared at him, for his words were a puzzlement.

Much about him puzzled her these days. He spoke to her little. His talk was mostly to her parents and about the war. But often, while he talked with them, she found him throwing quick glances at her. Yet he made no move to be with her alone so they might once again feel the closeness they had shared over the book.

Am I his secret, as he is mine? she wondered.

His visits were short, and each time he left she found herself hoping it would not be long until he returned. He brought no more books. Now he traded lead for Father's deerskins—the lead they melted into shot for the guns.

Just as well, Amity thought. The growing heaps of shot Father would take with him gave her a little hope for his safety.

There was small enough comfort in her thoughts these days. And at night, lying on her pallet in the loft, she tried to push away the dread scenes that leaped out of the dark.

Her mother shooting at foragers.

Her father shooting at soldiers.

Soldiers shooting at him.

On the evening before her father left, she held the last of the lead balls in her hand and looked down at the baby asleep in his cradle. Lucky little sweetling, she thought. Too young to know what leadshot does.

It might be better to be a child after all—nay, a baby like Jonathan. To know only about warmth and a full stomach, and nothing of armies and foragers and war.

CHAPTER

5

❖

Next morning, dew winked in the grass and the hills glowed with autumn colors, but Amity took no pleasure in such beauty. Dawn had come after a sleepless night. She rushed through morning chores but had no memory of doing them, and now breakfast was a swift, silent meal. Not even the soft cornmeal mush would go past the knot in her throat.

She watched her father sling his powder horn and shot pouch across his chest, shoulder his bedroll and towcloth bundle of clothes, and pick up his gun.

"It is time," he said, and nothing more. Everything else had been said during the days and evenings past.

Joanna Spencer lifted the baby from the cradle and wrapped him against the chill morning mist. With Ned beside them, they made their way down the hillpath to the road.

A small crowd of valley men waited, drawn up in straggling order. Amity was surprised to see how many there were. Tall, gruff Elias Nash, frowning as usual, was stamping his feet as if he couldn't wait to march away to fight Burgoyne. Karl Vrooman was beside him, a down-drooping look on his round, pleasant face, and nearby stood Dorf the miller, and his two tall sons, each with a bulging haversack on his back. Farmers from the western uplands were there too, the pockets of their homespun shirts stuffed with bread and cheese. Ben Tyler, looking older than his nineteen years, rested the butt of his gun on the ground and stared down at his feet. Ned bounded into the midst of the men, sniffing, leaping to friendly hands.

Amity was surprised to see Cheppa John. He was standing beside his wagon at a distance apart from them all. Dear Lord, does he mean to go too? she thought with a sudden pang. Three in danger—how can I bear it?

She wanted to run to him, but he was deep in talk with Isaac Thomas, who leaned heavily on a cane cut from a sapling and looked more ill than ever.

Polly waved and ran over to Amity. "We've been up for hours packing food!" she cried. "Flour, corncakes, cheese, and oh, so many sides of bacon! Matt says there's enough eating here for the whole army!"

A loaded wagon was hitched to Isaac Thomas's plowmare, and a pile of homespun blankets was tied across the horse's broad back. The old flintlock musket that had hung above the Thomases' hearth was strapped on as well.

"Pa said we ought to keep it, but Ma won't hear of it," Polly said. "She says she'd sooner chase off a forager with a broom than shoot that old musket. So off it goes with Matt, and some soldier without a gun can use it."

Matt carried his own gun. His deerhide cap sat jauntily on his red hair, and his eyes shone with excitement. When he caught sight of Amity, he made a show of marching over and saluting.

"Private Matthew Thomas reporting, ma'am," he said with a fancy salute. "Is General Burgoyne a bother to you? I'll thrash him at the first crossroads!"

Amity tried to smile, but today his joking sat wrong on her spirits. "Do take care, Matt," she said. "Try not to put yourself in the way of danger."

"Why, danger is what war is all about," he said. "But don't you worry about me—no, wait, *do* worry! That way I can tell Gentleman Johnny to treat me specially nice 'cause there's a lass back home all in a fret over me!"

He grinned down at her, but she could think of no way to answer. She turned to her father, but he was in quiet conversation with Mother. Wherever has Polly gone off to? she wondered, looking around.

There she was, smiling and chattering with the miller's sons, dancing her eyes prettily from one to the other, and showing no sign of coming back to Amity's side. Matt talked on, cheerful and bantering as usual, but Amity scarcely heard him.

Her thoughts were in a turmoil. How can you put Matt off this way? she scolded herself. He's going off to war, maybe to be killed. Tell him how dear he is to you, if not as husband, then as friend.

But the words would not come, and she could do nothing but look at him uncomfortably. And try to smile. And be glad when someone called him back to his place among the men.

Now here was Polly again, chattering over the mutter of men's voices. "See Master Jowdy!" she hissed into Amity's ear. "He must think he's going to a ball, not a war!"

The schoolmaster was turned out in a yellow coat and brown knee breeches. His gray hair was tied back with a shiny black ribbon, and a cockade of duck feathers perched on his three-cornered hat. He shouldered his musket awkwardly, but held himself straight and proud.

Polly looked longingly at the small group of men. "Oh, Amity, without Matt it'll be so dull here," she said. "I almost wish there *would* be foragers to chase away so we'd have something exciting to tell him when he comes back!"

Foolish Polly, Amity scolded silently. How wrongheaded it was to hope for danger. Yet, as she had many times before, Amity wished she could be like Polly—so cheerful, so sure that everything would turn out right and fine.

Polly flicked her eyes in the direction of the peddler. "Did you know Cheppa John stayed the night with us?" she whispered. "Pa had one of his bad times, couldn't sleep for coughing, and Cheppa John brewed him a posset and sat up with him at the hearth the whole night."

How like him, Amity thought.

"I heard their voices," Polly chattered on, "but I couldn't hear a word of their talk. Oh, I do hate sleeping up in a loft, don't you? Everything exciting goes on downstairs. I crept down the ladder once to listen, but Ma found me and chased me back. She didn't chase Matt, though."

"Matt?"

"He bedded down on the floor in front of the fire, would you believe such a thing? Said he ought to get used to a soldier's ways! There they all were when I came down this morning—Pa

44

in his chair and Matt on the floor wrapped in a quilt and Cheppa John stirring up the fire. I do think he . . ."

Her words were cut off by hoofbeats. A large gray horse galloped around the roadbend and reared up in front of the men, reined to a halt by its rider. Through the dust Amity caught a glimpse of a dark blue jacket with crisscrossed white straps, legs clad in buff leggings, and a club of sandy hair hanging beneath a black three-cornered hat.

She and Polly stared. A real soldier!

"Captain Francis Dunn, Continental Army," he called from his horse. "Here to escort you men to the army of General Horatio Gates."

"Isn't he handsome!" Polly breathed. Her eyes danced again, and she looked as if the miller's sons had no more room in her thoughts.

Amity guessed Polly hadn't noticed how thin and sleep-starved the captain looked. He was shabby too. His wrists stuck out of the frayed sleeves of his jacket and the white straps lying in an X on his chest were soiled, like the rest of his uniform.

"With a quick pace we can get halfway to Stillwater before sundown," Captain Dunn said. "We'll bed down overnight in a field and set sentries. Then on the morrow we'll march through Stillwater and upriver to the camp, where you will attach yourselves to the command of Major General Benedict Arnold."

Someone called, "What about you, peddler? Do you join us?"

Amity held her breath.

Cheppa John shook his head. "Nay," he called back. "A man of trade can be of better use than firing at redcoats."

45

What use would that be? Amity wondered. Wouldn't this Major General Benedict Arnold need every man to help him stand against Burgoyne's army?

There was an uncomfortable silence, a shuffling of feet. Then Elias Nash barked out a short laugh. "Aye, peddler, spread the word through the whole valley!" he shouted. "Rouse all the others from their firesides!"

Captain Dunn glanced at the women. "Say your farewells," he said. "Men, let's be off."

Amity felt her father's arm around her shoulders. "It will be a hard time for you and your mother," he said. "You must be each other's strength." He kissed her cheek and she clung to him, pushing tears down against the ache in her throat.

Now he drew her mother into the embrace too, kissed baby Jonathan, and held them all close as if he would memorize the very feel of them.

Matt ran over to give his mother a quick kiss and clasp his father's hand. He tweaked Polly's braids and said with a grin, "Let me hear of no trouble from you, miss. Amity, see that she doesn't go sneaking off to spy on the enemy! And remember your promise to worry about me!"

Again Amity tried to smile, but she could not force the pain out of her throat.

"Form ranks!" Captain Dunn ordered. Matt strode back to the knot of men, and Will Spencer took his place beside him.

Amity felt Polly clutch her arm. "Amity, look!" Polly whispered. "Captain Dunn is riding straight over to us!"

Through a haze of tears Amity saw the captain touch his hat politely to the women. "I trust you will be leaving the valley soon," he said.

Polly's eyelashes fluttered up at the captain. "We could go to my aunt's in Stillwater," she said, "if Ma would only—"

Joanna Spencer's words cut in. "I cannot speak for the Thomas family," she said, looking up at the man on the horse, "but my place is here."

Captain Dunn frowned. "A dangerous decision, ma'am," he said, "but your own to make, I warrant. In any case, burn your fields. General Gates wants not a single ear of corn left to feed Burgoyne's men."

Amity felt her mother stiffen. "You may tell General Gates that I will make quite sure no enemy soldier feeds off our land."

The captain followed her gesture to the thick trees that hid the farm. "Hill farmers, are you?" he said. "Well, you may be out of view from down here on the road, but Burgoyne's army is no stranger to woodland. You'd best lock yourselves in as much as you can, and your animals too. Hungry soldiers can smell a cow a mile off."

He wheeled his horse around, rode to the head of the group of men, and raised a hand high in the air. "Shoulder arms—march!" he said in a crisp voice.

"Pity we have no drummer boy," Schoolmaster Jowdy called out.

Elias Nash pounded his fist against the wagon's wooden sides. "I'll give us the beat," he shouted. "One—two! One—two!" They moved off to the bellow of his voice and the rhythmic thump of his fist.

Polly jumped up and down, waving and blowing kisses. "Farewell, farewell!" she shouted. "Matt—watch out for redcoats on the way!"

Matt grinned and waved, his chest thrust out as he strode along with the men. Amity strained to see them as long as she could, but soon the group was out of sight around the roadbend.

Mistress Thomas let her breath out in a heavy sigh. "They're gone," she said in a strangely flat voice.

"But it won't take them long to beat Gentleman Johnny!" Polly cried. "Soon they'll be home, and oh, I can't wait to hear Matt tell all about it!"

Mistress Thomas did not answer. Her face was as solemn as Joanna Spencer's own. She bent over the baby and kissed his forehead.

"Come along, Polly," she said as she straightened up. "Help your father into the house."

Amity scarcely saw them go for the tears clouding her eyes.

As if from a far distance she heard her mother call to Cheppa John. "Peddler, will you bide with us awhile?"

Cheppa John was already turning Toby and the wagon around. "Thank you, but nay," he called back over his shoulder. "I've business waiting. Mind you look to yourself, Mistress Spencer."

Amity felt his eyes on her. "Amity?" he called.

She turned back, trying to see through her tears. He made as if to move toward her, then stopped.

"Amity, take care," was all he said, but she felt his eyes burn into her.

The tinware on the wagon jangled as he climbed onto the high seat and set Toby to a slow jog. Now it seemed a joyless sound. Amity took her mother's arm, and together they walked slowly up the hillpath. Behind them was nothing but a swirl of dust settling to the empty road.

CHAPTER

6

❖

The days crawled past, filled with worry and work. Nights, with their scaredreams, were worse. Amity no longer slept in the loft, alone. When the evening was done, the baby asleep in his cradle, and the hearth embers made ready for the morning's fire, she and her mother huddled together in the big rope bed in the sleeping room downstairs. Together they lay listening to night sounds, glad of the fowling gun and shot pouch Father had left them, wondering if they might some day, some night, have to use it.

In the mornings, as Amity pulled on her clothes, she caught a glimpse of her face in the small mirror nailed to the wall near the bed.

Such a plain face, she thought. It had none of Polly's vivid brightness, no sparkling brown eyes, no freckles sprinkled across an uptilted nose. And none of Charity Tyler's soft beauty lit by pale yellow hair and eyes the color of flax blossoms. The best the mirror could show was light brown hair, light brown eyes. In my light brown shawl, Amity thought, I must look like one of the wrens that nest under the cowshed roof.

Still, something in her had caught Cheppa John's interest.

Her face burned where he had touched it, and as she tied the drawstring at the neck of her shift she peered more closely into the mirror. She had her mother's wide-browed, even features and clear skin. Maybe some day she'd be as pretty as Joanna Spencer had been, not so long ago.

She tucked her hair under the white mobcap and tied her apron over her dress. Stop mooning about your looks, she scolded herself. Yet she knew she'd keep on. These frivolous moments pushed aside the thoughts of Father and Matt in danger, of herself and Mother and baby Jonathan so alone each day, each night.

She invented many ways to stop her fearful imaginings. She made up foolish little baby songs, gently clapping Jonathan's small hands together as she sang to him. Over and over again she told him the story of Robin Hood, for the book Cheppa John had given her sat firm in her memory from many readings. As she churned or spun or scrubbed the plank table, she bent over the cradle and sang or chattered to him, and it seemed as if the sound of her voice made a warm shelter for them both.

But fearsome images lay underneath, waiting to catch her without warning. One night she jerked awake screaming. Her mother's arms went around her instantly.

"What is it, child?"

"Father! I saw him! There were Tories behind bushes, and soldiers—redcoats pointing their guns at him, and cannons too, and he had only a small musket no bigger than a spindle, and ..."

Her mother soothed her down under the quilt, but sleep was long in coming again, and when it did it brought back bits of the dream.

She knew her mother had scaredreams too, for often their shadows lay on her face in the morning. It had been more than two weeks since the men left, and there had been no word.

Why do we hear nothing from Cheppa John? Amity wondered. Has he changed his mind and gone off to the fighting after all? She trembled to think of it.

Mornings were colder now. Each day Amity wrapped her shawl close around her as she hurried to the cowshed. Each day her mother watched from the doorway as she had never done before. One misty morning her mother called after her, "Remember not to linger. And keep Ned by your side."

As if she needed to be told. Whenever she went the smallest distance outside, she made sure Ned was close beside her.

This morning she had not been long at the milking when Ned's ears rose. He leaped up and ran barking toward the hill-path, and Amity jumped away from Lady. Should she race after him or make for the house? He had not snarled, so whoever was coming must be someone he knew. Someone like . . .

"Father!"

But the man trudging heavy-footed up the hill was not her father. It was Ben Tyler, his arm bound up in a bloody bandage. He walked as if a burden lay on his back, although he carried nothing but his gun.

"Good news!" he shouted when he saw her. "We met the enemy in battle, and your father is safe!"

Safe! The word leaped into every corner of the room as Amity watched Ben gulp down a steaming bowl of cabbage soup. She and her mother could scarce take their eyes from him. Hungry as he was, it was nothing like their own hunger for news.

"He said to tell you he's unharmed and well," Ben said between swallows. "And he thinks of you always and trusts you're well and safe too."

Amity felt a stone lift from her chest. Her mother's face took on a faint color, and she seemed to be smiling as she set bread in front of Ben. He ate as if he'd seen no food for days, head bent over the bowl, eyes looking only at the table.

Amity sank down near him. "Tell us about Matt too," she said anxiously. "Is he safe, like Father? And the others—are they unharmed too? Tell us how you got wounded. Is the pain bad?"

Ben pushed his bowl across the table. "Mistress Spencer, can you spare more soup?" he asked.

Amity went on impatiently. "Did you see Cheppa John? Did he join up with the rest of you? What was it like in camp? Oh, Ben, tell us everything!"

"Hush, Amity, let the lad fill his stomach," her mother said. "And fetch clean linen so I can tend to his arm. We mustn't send him on to Charity with a wound that might fester."

Amity ran for the linen, not wanting to miss a word Ben might say. But he said nothing, and when she came back he was still bent over his soup. Talk! she said silently to his back. Tell us! Then, remembering the ragged man's hunger, she bit back her impatience.

Unlike the ragged man, Ben didn't seem eager to talk when he finished eating. He pushed away from the table and walked to the hearthfire, frowning down at the flames.

"Did we win the battle?" Amity burst out.

Ben shook his head. "It can't be called a victory for either side," he said. "Burgoyne is halted, but not turned back. He's made camp at Freeman's farm, where the fighting was, and our troops are settling in behind log barricades. Word has it that he may attack again, but no one knows."

Amity saw the light go out of her mother's face. "More fighting," Joanna Spencer said.

"No one knows," Ben said again, still looking down. "If there's a long stalemate, Burgoyne may have to pull back to Fort Ti for the winter. Our spies tell us his supplies are low."

"Spies!" Amity felt a twist of excitement.

Ben looked up now and began talking fast, his words spilling into each other. "Aye, both sides have spies aplenty, and couriers to carry secret messages. Just before the battle, our men captured a Tory with a letter from Burgoyne, and where do you think the man had hidden it? Inside a silver bullet! No one would have known, but when they took him to General Gates he pulled the bullet out of his shot pouch and put it in his mouth and swallowed it down!"

"Swallowed it!"

"Aye, and a fair lot of commotion there was till he was made to vomit it up," Ben went on.

Amity felt her own stomach lurch. She turned away.

"It saved the trouble of cutting it out of his stomach after he was hanged," Ben said. "Hanged on the spot he was, while we all watched—not a pretty sight. Aye, spying's a dirty business."

Joanna Spencer set a basin of water on the table with a loud thump. "Sit down, Ben," she said. "Let me look at this wound."

He sat, and she began to unwrap the bandage. Her touch was gentle, but he winced as she pulled at the blood-caked cloth. Still, he poured out more and more words and Amity peered at him curiously. She had never known Ben Tyler to talk so much. It was as if he were building a barricade of words around himself.

She drew her chair closer. "Tell us about the battle," she said. "No, tell us what it was like in camp. No, first tell us about Father and the others."

A smile began on his face. "You sound like your skitterwit friend Polly," he said, and as soon as the words were said, the smile disappeared. He shifted uneasily and glanced aside.

Why won't he look at me? she wondered. It's as if he's hiding something. But if Father's safe, and Matt, and the others, what could there be to hide?

He slid quick words into the silence. "The camp was hasty built," he said. "Tents and lean-tos all over, and mud, and so much noise! Drums beating and soldiers drilling, and officers on horse-back galloping in and out. Men like us came legging in from all over the countryside, and a good thing too, for a draggle-tailed army it is. No uniforms for the Regulars, just for the officers, and not enough food or medicine, and hardly enough guns or powder or shot."

Joanna Spencer sighed heavily. "It's as I feared," she said. "We are too weak to defeat Burgoyne."

"But we have Morgan's riflemen!" Ben said, and for a moment his eyes shone.

"Who?"

"The best fighters in the whole Continental Army! Backwoodsmen from Virginia and Kentucky, and what a sight they are, in buckskin breeches and coon fur caps with the tails still on 'em!"

As Amity tried to picture such a sight, Ben went on in a rush. "Got their own leader, Colonel Daniel Morgan. The talk around camp was that General Washington specially pulled them away from his own army and sent them up to go against Burgoyne. The British fear Morgan's men like the devil's own."

"Why?" Amity asked.

"It's the way they shoot," Ben said. "Any one of them can punch the core out of an apple or bring down a redcoat at three hundred yards. Everyone says so!"

"That cannot be!" Amity's mother protested. "No one can shoot such a far distance!"

"*They* can," Ben insisted. "Those guns of theirs are as long as a man is tall, with ridges inside the barrels. Rifling, they call it, and it makes the guns shoot straighter than any other. Aye, a man

56

with a good eye and one of those long rifles will hit the mark every time!"

It was hard for Amity to imagine shooting that never missed. Even her father often failed to bring down deer with his musket.

Now Ben's face was lit with excitement. Amity was glad to see that whatever had sorrowed him before was gone.

"Tell us more about the riflemen," she begged.

"Well, they can shoot fast too," Ben said. "They carry their leadshot right in the hollow butts of the rifles—each ball wrapped in a patch of buckskin soaked in bear grease, so it'll ram down quick. Aye, quick as I can tell you, any one of them can shoot the whiskers off a squirrel and then load again and pot a redcoat square between the eyes!"

Joanna Spencer flinched, but Amity had caught Ben's excitement. "How fine!" she cried. "If only our whole army had rifles!"

Ben shook his head. "You can't have just riflemen," he said. "An army needs its musketmen, because . . ."

He stopped. "Why?" Amity pressed.

"Because a rifle's too long and thin to . . . well, you can't hitch a bayonet on it," he went on. "And a man without a bayonet can't . . . can't defend himself when the fighting gets close. Or if he's . . . downed by a shot and . . . and left on the field."

His voice trailed off and he brushed a hand over his eyes.

Amity searched for something to say. "How Matt must admire those riflemen! And Polly—oh, I hope you told the Thomases about them—I can just see Polly's face!"

Ben was silent. "I haven't been to the Thomases," he said at last, and something in his voice made Joanna Spencer look up from winding a clean cloth around his arm.

"Why not?" she asked. "Their farm lies nearer the road than ours."

"I . . . couldn't," Ben said, and he turned away as if he could not bear to meet her eyes.

In the silence Amity stared from Ben to her mother. Joanna Spencer's face had gone white.

Ben forced himself to speak. "I . . . thought to come here first, ma'am," he said slowly, "and ask if you would go with me. The fact is, I must tell them it's likely Matt is . . . Matt was . . . killed."

Amity heard two strange, faraway voices cry out "No!" One, she realized, was her own.

Now she knew why Ben's eyes had slid around the room so, why he had looked everywhere except straight into her face.

Matt. Dear Matt.

"I'll tell Gentleman Johnny to treat me specially nice," he had said. She remembered the foolish salute he had given her, his grin and wave as he marched away with the men, the youngest of them all. How open-faced and fearless he'd been as he'd gone off to the war.

Matt killed. She could scarce believe that mere words could bring such pain.

As if from a far distance she heard her mother drag out a whisper. "You'd best tell us what happened."

Ben struggled to find his own voice. Then at last, slowly now, the words came.

"We were all together when the fighting started—Master Jowdy and your husband, ma'am, and Matt and the others, all of us working to build a barricade on the north side of the camp. Along about midday we heard shooting from far off, and up rode General Arnold. 'Take up your guns, boys, and follow me!' he shouted, and we did, and he was like a wild man, galloping about on his big horse, shouting orders, leading us straight to a cornfield full of redcoats."

Amity saw it all in his words—her father, Matt, the others, running across land meant for farming, not killing.

"They came at us across that field like a red wall," Ben went on, "shoulder to shoulder, with fire blazing out of their muskets. I scarce knew what to do, specially when some of our men went down. It was all a terrible muddle, but Arnold was there, leading us on as if we had been soldiering all our lives. 'Fire!' he yelled, and we fired, and a lot of redcoats went down, but the rest just stepped over them as if they were only fallen logs. They kept on coming, and some were shooting and some were pointing their bayonets straight at us, and all I wanted to do was throw down my gun and run off."

Ben stopped. He rubbed a hand over his eyes.

"I hadn't expected the screaming," he said at last. "I was ready for drums beating signals and the way musket fire crackles and the roar cannons make—I'd heard Regulars talk about all that in camp. But not the screaming. The way men sound wh-when leadshot tears into them. And horses. I . . . never heard a horse scream before."

"Oh, Ben," Amity heard her mother breathe.

"Maybe I screamed too when I got hit—I don't remember. All I know is I went down, and all around me were bodies, and the cornstalks were red and slippery with blood and somebody was dragging me away. The next thing I knew, I was back in camp and your husband, ma'am, was tending me, and night was coming down."

"And . . . Matt?" Amity's mother asked.

Ben stared into the fire. "Nowhere to be found," he answered. "Not in our hospital tents, not anywhere. Master Jowdy and the others searched the whole camp."

"He was left on the battlefield wounded!" Amity cried. "Why did no one go back for him?"

"Some tried," Ben said, "but the redcoats held the field and had sentries posted all over. It would have been death to keep on."

There was silence.

"Left to die in the dark," Joanna Spencer said in a small, flat voice. "And his . . . body?"

Ben swallowed hard. "The dead had to be buried fast," he said. "Thrown into big pits, whether British or American, and covered with earth and stones against the wolves."

"Wolves!" Amity's hand flew to her mouth.

"Packs of them," Ben went on. "They'd followed Burgoyne's army all those miles through the wilderness, feeding on the army's leavings and . . ."

Again silence. "And on soldiers dead of disease. And now, after the battle, they . . . smelled the blood and came out of the woods. All night they prowled around, so close you could see their eyes glow in the cookfires. Master Jowdy said Matt and the other dead were . . . lucky to have been given so quick a burial."

There was silence again. "There will not be much comfort for his family in that," Joanna Spencer said at last.

"Aye," Ben agreed with a heavy sigh. "Nor in this scrap I'm to take back to them."

With his good arm he drew out of his pocket a crumpled deerskin cap. "It was all of Matt could be found."

Amity stared at the torn, stained cap, and the images sprang again out of her memory—Matt grinning as he marched off with the menfolk, his eyes bright with excitement, his red hair curling around the edges of that very cap.

She searched for a wisp of hope. "What if . . . maybe he's not dead at all. He could have been taken prisoner."

Ben shook his head. "Burgoyne takes no prisoners. He can't spare food for them, or men to guard them."

"But . . ."

"No prisoners," Ben insisted. "We all know that for certain. Morgan sent out scouts, and they came back with word that after the battle the British went around with bayonets and . . . and finished off any of our wounded left on the field. If some-body hadn't dragged me away, I'd likely be in a deadpit now."

Amity turned aside. "I'm glad you're alive, Ben," she said in a voice she could hardly hear. "And Father."

But Matt . . .

Oh, Matt.

Her mother sat silent and pale, hands clasped to her lips. At last, with a slow shake of her head, she bent to the cradle, lifted out the baby, and wrapped the quilt around him.

"Come, both of you," she said as she moved toward the door. "We have a sorrowful task to do."

CHAPTER

7

❖

Days passed, but the pain did not. Amity was wrenched back to the misery that had wracked her when Simon died.

She dreaded visiting the Thomases now. Isaac Thomas sat wrapped in grief, his head sunk on his chest, and Mistress Thomas rarely spoke. Her bustling cheerfulness was gone, replaced by deep shuddering sighs as she went slowly about her tasks, stopping sometimes to pat her husband's thin hand or sit silently beside him.

There was no silence in Polly. "I hate the war!" she shouted, stamping restlessly about the room where once she had marched, laughing, with a broom on her shoulder. "I hate Burgoyne! I hate every soldier in his army, and every one of his spies, and every Tory who aids him, and . . . oh, I hate them all!"

Amity wanted to put her arms around her and cry, but Polly was snappish and impatient. The laughter in her had sputtered out like a candle stub. Now she was all anger, blazing at everything.

"I hate being on this hateful farm in this hateful war!" she burst out one day. "There's nothing to do but milk and churn and look after smelly, witless, *hateful* animals."

"Get on with your chores, Polly," Mistress Thomas said with a sigh. "In war, men fight and women suffer at home."

No! Amity wanted to shout. It isn't enough to suffer at home. A person must act, even if that person *is* only a woman. She longed to do something—anything—that would help bring Father home safely.

But there was nothing to do except plod on through each day.

In the long evenings, spinning or sewing near the hearthfire, Amity argued with herself about Matt.

I shouldn't have pushed aside his marriage talk, she thought. I should have let him have his dream—the two of us working his farm, raising a flock of red-haired children, living the cycles of planting and reaping as the years creep on.

But that was *his* dream, a voice in her answered back. What of mine? What of books to read and places to go and people to meet? What of being wife to Cheppa John?

There had been no sign of Cheppa John for weeks. Where is he? she wondered anxiously. Is he safe? Does he know about Matt? Before the invasion there had been little the peddler didn't know, but now everything was a muddle. The men were gone and most of the women too, and everyone's life was a heap of scraps.

Scraps—like the patchquilt she was struggling to make for Jonathan. One evening, as she pieced together the points of a star, Amity frowned at the crooked wanderings of her stitches.

"Here's a whole square to be ripped out," she said, sounding as impatient as Polly.

"Leave it be," her mother said. "Thread is precious. We'll have no more till Cheppa John comes."

The sound of his name lifted Amity's spirits. "Where do you suppose he is?" she said. "Downriver getting other men to join against Burgoyne?"

"It might be," her mother answered.

"Or soldiering with Father and the others in camp?" Amity went on. "Maybe he means to set aside peddling until Burgoyne is beaten."

"Beaten? How?" Joanna Spencer's quiet voice was bitter.

"The riflemen," Amity offered hopefully. "Ben said . . ."

Her mother's lips pressed together and cut off any more talk. Amity saw how the hearthlight flickering over her face lit lines never there before. Since the news of Matt's death Joanna Spencer had kept her thoughts locked inside, but each day she attacked her tasks harder, as if work could erase sorrow and worry.

Amity searched for something else to say about Cheppa John, needing to say his name. Needing to turn the talk away from the war.

"If Cheppa John should come by," she said, trying to sound cheerful, "do you suppose I might have some real buttons for my dress? White bone, or maybe even pewter? Charity had silver ones on her dress when she married Ben. Cheppa John brought them all the way from Albany."

Foolish, jibbering talk, she thought. A dress to be wed in was special, and Charity Bates's family was well able to afford silver buttons. How lovely Charity had looked in her blue linsey-woolsey dress with its lace collar and delicate silver buttons.

Amity fingered the large buttons on her bodice. They were covered with homespun, and they faded into the dress as if they weren't even there. She knew she would likely not have any other kind. Town-made buttons were fripperies. Homespun stitched over wooden forms did just as well for farm girls.

Her mother gave the answer she'd been expecting. "Best stop yearning for fancy buttons, child," she said. "We have nothing to spare in trade. We'll need every scrap of food if . . . if the war drags into winter."

And if Father doesn't come home, Amity thought.

She jabbed her needle into the quilt. If only this miserable evening would end.

Later, as she tried to settle herself for sleep, she wondered again about Cheppa John. Had he gone off to soldier with the others? What, then, had he done with the wagon? Where had he left Toby?

It was near October now—why had he sent no word? Had he forgotten her? Huddled next to her mother, she stared into the darkness until sleep finally came.

Early the next morning the loud bleating of sheep woke them both.

Amity's heart thudded. "Someone's broken into the cowshed—they're driving off the sheep!" she whispered.

They pulled on their shoes and hurried to the door. As her mother gripped the gun, Amity slowly drew back the bolt and opened the door a crack.

Sheep, confused and complaining, were scrambling up the hillpath toward the house. In their midst were Mistress Thomas and Polly, prodding them with sticks.

Amity stood staring in amazement. "Why—?" she began.

"Hush, child," her mother said. "Open the pasture gate." She put an arm around Mistress Thomas and led her toward the house.

Amity rushed to help Polly pen the sheep in the pasture. "What is happening?" she whispered.

"We're moving to Stillwater," Polly whispered back. "Ma says we can't stay here any longer."

"Oh, no!" Amity cried.

Polly was pale under her freckles, but there was a flash of excitement in her eyes. "Ma says it's only for a while," she said. "Oh, Amity, it's just what I've wanted!"

Amity turned away and walked slowly toward the house. Inside, Mistress Thomas sat on the high-backed settle, her plump face sagging. For a moment she smiled into the cradle, but it was a small, bleak smile that faded almost as soon as it began.

Her voice trembled as she spoke. "Isaac is ailing worse every day," she said. "Since the news about Matt . . ."

She looked away, clasping and unclasping her hands. "Doctoring is what he needs, and he'll get it in Stillwater at my sister Kate's. And besides . . . with our house so close to the road . . . if enemy raiders come, I don't know what I'd . . ."

67

Her words stumbled on and Amity listened numbly, wanting not to hear.

"You'll be alone here, Joanna, you and the young ones, but . . ." Her voice trailed off and she buried her face in her hands. "We can't stay, we can't," she sobbed.

Over Mistress Thomas's bowed head Amity looked at her mother and saw the struggle in her face.

"When will you leave?" Joanna Spencer said.

"Tomorrow," Mistress Thomas answered.

And the next morning Amity found herself once more standing at the roadside choking over words of farewell.

The Thomases' cow had been hitched to a small cart, and Isaac Thomas was wedged in among bundles and sacks. He sat silent, staring off into nothing.

Polly threw her arms around Amity. "It's just for a visit," she said. "When Burgoyne is turned back for good and Aunt Kate has nursed my father well again, then we'll come home, and I'll tell you all about Stillwater."

But Amity, looking at the Thomas house with its shutters nailed tight and its sheep pen empty, wondered if Polly would come back after all. It seemed more likely that she would beg to stay in town. If they ever saw each other again, likely Polly would be married, if not to one of Dorf the miller's sons, then to a shopkeeper or an innkeeper. Anyone but a farmer.

Amity pulled herself back to the present. "Where will you stay this night?" she managed to ask.

"Ma says the Prestons will give us shelter, midway between

here and Stillwater. And tomorrow we'll be at Aunt Kate's, and—oh, Amity, think of it! I'll be a town girl! No more farm chores!"

Amity forced herself to fall in with Polly's cheerfulness. "Captain Dunn said the Continentals' camp is close to Stillwater," she said. "You might see soldiers in the town."

"Oh, I hope so!" Polly said. "And there will be ladies buying bonnets and supplies in Aunt Kate's shop, and—"

"Shop?" Amity said in surprise.

"Didn't you know? Uncle Edward was a shopkeeper till he died of the pox. The shop is part of Aunt Kate's house. Oh, Amity, it will be so different from this dreary old farm."

Polly chattered on while the two mothers stood close together, murmuring quietly, wiping away tears.

"It pains me to think of you and the children so alone here," Amity heard Mistress Thomas say again. "But we must go."

She saw her mother nod, heard her say, "I understand, Nell. Don't fret about us."

Not a word was said of Matt, but his image lay before them all.

Then they were off. Polly and her mother walked beside the cow, looking back and waving, but Isaac Thomas was so sunk into himself that he gave no sign of farewell. Watching them go, Amity felt new misery rub sore against the old. At the roadbend Polly turned and blew her a kiss, but Amity could only manage a small wave in return.

The wolf came two nights later. They did not know it was a

wolf, only that something roused Ned to barking and sent Amity's mother running to the door with the gun. In the moonlight there was nothing to be seen, and when daylight came, no tracks of animal or human. Still, there had been something outside the house.

In the morning Joanna Spencer slung the shot bag and powder horn across her chest and picked up the gun. "We'll go to morning chores together," she said.

Amity looked back at the cradle. "But . . ."

"He'll be safe," her mother said, "as long as we are. Come." She stepped over the doorsill, holding the gun to her shoulder.

With Ned beside them they made their way slowly toward the cowshed. It was a damp, rain-misted dawn, but the chill that licked at Amity's neck had nothing to do with the cold autumn air.

Suddenly Ned stopped, and Amity saw his fur rise. He pushed against them, herding them back. Out of the shadows of the cowshed sprang a dark gray form that flung Ned down on his back. Ned was a big dog and strong, but the wolf, a snarling streak of fur with snapping yellow teeth, was bigger still.

"Mother—shoot!" Amity shrieked.

But Joanna Spencer, gun to her shoulder, stood frozen. The leadshot would tear into Ned as well, for he and the wolf were locked into one snarling, spinning mass.

Amity looked around frantically for something, anything that would separate the fighting animals. A length of fence rail leaned against the cowshed, and she snatched it up.

"Amity! No!" her mother screamed, but there was a moment when the wolf sank its jaws into Ned's leg and Ned, yelping with pain, went flat in the dust. With all her strength Amity thrust the rail at the wolf's gray haunches.

Again.

Again.

The wolf pitched sideways, scrambled up, and leaped at her.

Then the gun roared, and what had been bloody teeth and claws and rough gray fur flying at her was suddenly a torn carcass on the ground. Twitching, then still.

Amity felt her mother's arm around her. For a moment they clung to each other, trembling. Then, with shaky hands, Joanna Spencer reloaded the gun, set it down carefully, and knelt beside Ned.

"Water," she said, as she tore off her apron and pressed the cloth to Ned's wounds. "Be quick."

Amity tried not to look at the dead wolf as she stumbled to the well. She hauled up a bucket of water and set it down beside her mother.

Oh, poor Ned, she thought. Brave Ned. She meant to say the words aloud, but couldn't push them out of her mouth. Her heart was pounding, her stomach churning, and the roar of the gun still thundered in her head.

At last Joanna Spencer stood up. "We must bury the wolf," she said. "The smell of blood might draw others."

Amity shuddered, remembering what Ben had told them about wolves following Burgoyne's army. Had they now spread over the whole valley? Were there others here now, lurking about the farm? She spun around, looking swiftly past the fields and the pasture, squinting into the woods.

Nothing there.

Not yet.

"Amity?" Her mother's voice seemed to come from far away. "Child, bring an empty grain sack from the cowshed."

When she unlocked the shed, she found Lady and Jess moving about nervously. "Hush now," Amity soothed as she ran her hand over their restless flanks. "Everything's fine. Wait till Ned tells you how brave he was."

How like Simon that sounds, she thought. Simon had always talked to the animals as if they were human and would speak right back to him. What would Simon do now? she wondered. Would he shrink from whatever had to be done with that bloody mass of fur and teeth out there?

She gave Lady and Jess a last pat. "Everything's fine," she said again, as much to comfort herself as to calm them.

Her mother gave her a searching look as she brought the sack. "There's time enough for the wolf," Joanna Spencer said. "We'll look to Ned first. Help me move him."

Gently, mindful that in his pain he might snap at them, they rolled Ned onto the sack and dragged him into the house. They settled him in front of the hearthfire, where he lay whimpering softly.

"Stay, Ned," Amity told him, even though he showed no sign of moving. She wished she could stay there with him.

"Amity," her mother said. "Come, child. It must be done."

Her stomach squeezed up into her throat. She gulped, then followed her mother back outside.

They used the same sack. Grunting, panting, sweating in the cold morning air, they dragged the wolf to a gully beyond the pasture and heaved it in, bloody sack and all. They threw rocks and earth and leaves over it, then trudged back to the farmyard and scraped earth over the blood-soaked ground in front of the cowshed.

They did it all silently, and when it was done Joanna Spencer straightened up and looked at Amity.

"Well done," she said with a nod, and only later did Amity notice that she had not called her "child."

CHAPTER

8

❖

No more wolves came, but fear locked tight around the hillfarm.

Amity began to understand her mother's need for work. She polished pewter plates that didn't need polishing, pulled wool through the carding paddles long after it was smooth enough for spinning. While her mother tended the baby, she tended Ned.

Simon, am I doing it as well as you would? she asked silently each time she saw to the dog.

Simon had had a gift with animals. "Never saw anything the way animals take to this lad," Father had once said. Amity remembered the time Ned had treed a baby raccoon, and Simon had climbed up and caught it. How it did scratch him! But he made a pet of it and got it to eat out of his hand, and . . .

She bit off the memory. After Simon died, Mother had opened the coon's pen and chased it back to the woods. Without a word.

Ned stayed indoors now, limping and weak. Most of the time he lay near the hearthfire or under the table, head down, tail still.

"Each day he seems a bit stronger, doesn't he?" Amity said, hoping it was true.

Her mother nodded, but slowly. Was it only a hope for her too?

They never talked about the wolf. Often, though, in the evenings, Amity would glance up from her lapwork and see her mother looking at her in a strange new way. If only I could know what she is thinking, Amity fretted.

She shook herself angrily. She felt penned in by if-only's. If only Matt had not been killed. If only Polly were still here. If only Burgoyne would be defeated and Father would come home.

If only Cheppa John would come.

She found it hard to sit quietly and sew. The pieces of the patchquilt came together even more crooked, for she was too restless to set them neatly. One evening, when the thread tangled and she jerked at it so hard that it broke, she threw the work down.

Her mother looked up from the crying baby. "Spinning will help," she said.

It was true. Spinning was move-about work—stepping forward, stepping back, using feet and hands to keep the wool moving smoothly on the large wheel, letting the rhythm of the work demand and soothe at the same time.

Amity tried to clear her thoughts of all but the rattle of the wheel and the feel of the wool pulling between her fingers onto the spindle. Spin steady, spin smooth, she told herself as she walked back and forth, back and forth, keeping to the pace of the wheel. Steady, smooth, steady.

The baby gave a loud, long wail and she turned to look anxiously at him. His small face was red and crinkled with distress. The cradle jiggled as, with sharp cries, he drew up his legs and kicked them straight again.

"Don't fuss, Jonathan," Amity begged him. "Mother and I worry when you fuss."

He had been fretful for several days. Her mother had dosed him with wormwood and sweet basil, but he seemed no better. Now, as her mother picked him up again and pressed his hot face against her cheek, Amity saw new worry lines in her tired face.

What if he should truly sicken? It was a new, jolting fear. Amity thought of the two small wooden headstones in the clearing at the side of the house. What if this third infant were as frail as the others?

If only Cheppa John would come, she thought again. He had remedies learned from his father—plant juices and seed oils, special herbs ground to powder, roots that brewed up into healing teas. Once he had dosed her through quinsy with herb possets and a poultice that drew the fever out. She remembered how he had stayed until her fever broke, how he had made jests to take her thoughts off the pain in her throat.

And how he had struggled with tears, years later, when his remedies had not kept Simon alive.

Where is he? she wondered for the thousandth time. What has kept him away these many weeks?

"Mind, Amity, the yarn grows lumpy!" her mother warned sharply. Amity jumped. Off in her thoughts, she had lost the rhythm, and the long twist of wool had gone slack. She took a firmer hold on the wool and gave the wheel an angry push. At least I must do this one task right, she thought.

A growl from Ned made her jump again. He was limping to the door, growling, the fur on his neck bristling. Amity jerked the wheel to a stop.

Another wolf?

Swiftly her mother put the baby back in his cradle and took up the gun. Amity ran to the window and peered into the dusk through a chink in the shutter. A shadowy form moved behind a clump of bushes.

It was no wolf, no animal of any kind. In the near darkness she could see cloth, and a glint of metal.

Her stomach knotted and her mouth went dry. Worse than a wolf, then. A forager. Or an enemy scout. Or a deserter from one of the armies—starving, desperate, wild to break in.

Over the baby's wails she heard her mother's voice. "What is it, Amity?"

"I . . . I can't tell," she said. "I think . . . it seems to be a man."

"Are there others?"

"I don't know—it's too dark to see."

She steadied herself against the edge of the shutter. Deserters travel alone, her mother had told her, but foragers would come in bands. A deserter might want only food and shelter, and then be on his way at dawnlight, but foragers . . .

One or many? she wondered. And what will they do? Break

open the cowshed and steal the animals? Or hurl themselves against the door of the house, break the wooden bar to splinters, and burst in with muskets and bayonets? Take every scrap of food, then leave the three of us dead?

"Amity!" Her mother stood at the door, gun ready, waiting. "How many?"

She strained to see into the shadows, pressing her face so close to the shutter that the wood bit into her cheek. "Only the one . . . I think."

It *was* only one, a crouching figure that suddenly swayed forward and staggered out of the bushes. His arms flailed, as if he had no balance, and his head was thrust forward so that . . .

Amity gasped. It couldn't be.

And yet . . . there! Once again—a flash of red hair.

"I think . . . yes, it's Matt!"

She ran past her mother, heaved up the heavy wooden bolt, and swung the door open. "Matt? Is it you?"

He gave no answer, but lurched over the doorsill, crumpled, and fell. He lay still as death, as his blood oozed onto the floorboards in dark splotches.

His clothes were caked with mud, tattered to shreds. His face was so crusted with scratches, his lips so cracked and swollen, that Amity could hardly recognize him. But it *was* Matt, and she felt joy rush over her in a great wave. "He's alive!" she cried, and hugged the very word to herself, saying it over and over again, feeling it ring through her whole body.

"Alive!" Joanna Spencer echoed, her own joy clear in her

voice. She laid the gun aside and knelt close to him, peering at his torn, bloody face.

"We must get him to the hearthlight," she said. "Slowly— take care, Amity. His pain must be fearsome."

As they dragged him across the room, Amity stumbled on a tangled leather strap. Something had fallen to the floor with him—a strange object round as a plate but thick, and made of leather.

"Bother!" she said, and kicked it out of the way. Ned growled, then dragged it under the table and began to chew on it.

By the time they got Matt to the hearth, he had opened his eyes. Joanna Spencer held a cup of water to his lips and he managed a few sips.

"What a fearful state he's in," Amity heard her mother say. "Light more candles, Amity, and bring them close."

Gently she pulled away the torn, bloodstained clothing. Amity winced. He was covered with deep, jagged wounds. Worst of all was one leg, torn thigh to ankle in great gashes.

In the yellow light of the candles she watched her mother bend over Matt's leg. "I see no sign of a lead ball," Joanna Spencer said at last, "but this is a dreadful wound."

"A bayonet!" Amity said. "Remember what Ben Tyler said about Burgoyne's men after the battle? How they went about killing the wounded Americans with their bayonets? Well . . ." She gulped. "Well, they didn't kill Matt! He managed to crawl away!"

Her mother shook her head. "It cannot be," she said. "The

battle was weeks ago, yet this is no old wound broken open. It's fresh, and too jagged to have been made by a bayonet. It's as if some wild creature has torn at him, and—"

A loud wail from the cradle cut off her words.

Amity turned and scooped up the baby. "Look, Jonathan—Matt's alive!" she crooned. "Isn't that the loveliest thing ever?"

She dipped a wad of clean linen into a bowl of honey water and held it to his mouth. As he sucked at it and was quiet, she smiled down at him.

She had a smile for Ned too, chewing busily under the table, the leather strap dangling from his mouth.

"See, Ned—Matt's alive!" she said. She felt like twirling about in a wild dance. Like Polly. Oh, if only Polly and her family were here now!

Or Cheppa John, to carry the wondrous news to Stillwater: "Listen, everyone—Matt is alive!"

Joanna Spencer worked over Matt for a long time. She cleaned the ugly gashes in his leg and bandaged them, smoothed salve over the angry red cuts that covered him. Amity rocked the baby in her arms, then gentled him into the cradle. She turned back to Matt and couldn't help beaming at him. His eyes were open but she wasn't sure he saw her.

"Amity, fetch your pallet from the loft," Joanna Spencer said at last.

Amity raced up the ladder. She dragged down the pallet and they managed to roll him onto it. Amity winced to hear him groan.

"A pillow for his head," her mother said. "Hurry."

At last Matt seemed to be more comfortable. Joanna Spencer put a bowl of the baby's gruel to his lips. He grunted, then gulped it hungrily.

Amity smiled at him. "Seems like you haven't eaten in days, Matt Thomas," she said. "Where have you been? What has happened to you?"

Through swollen lips he began to speak, croaking out words in a voice so hoarse that they had to bend close to hear.

"Home . . . no one . . . where are they?" He waved an arm weakly in the direction of the farm down the hill.

"They're in Stillwater, Matt," Joanna Spencer said. "Gone to stay with your aunt Kate for a while. How happy they'll be to know you're safe." Gently she tucked a quilt around him. "Rest now. Later you'll tell us what happened."

No! Amity wanted to shout. Tell it now! But she held her tongue and watched him sink slowly into sleep.

Now there was nothing to do but wait. And work, to keep her hands busy while her head fought back the burning wonder about where he had been and what had happened to him. She gathered bloody cloths and put them to soak in a crock of water. "What of these?" she asked, holding up Matt's ruined shirt and breeches. "They're past mending. Shall we burn them?"

Her mother shook her head. "When the blood has come out, we'll see what small thing we can make of the cloth." Into the crock they went, and the swirl of red water made Amity's stomach move uneasily.

Floorboards next. Together they scrubbed at the bloodstains with sand and soap. So much blood these past days, Amity thought.

But Matt's alive!

Ned nuzzled against her, dragging the round leather object by its strap. Amity gave him a gentle push. "Away from this clean floor," she said. "And don't chew on Matt's shot pouch. He'll not want it ruined when . . ."

She sat back on her heels. "Wait, let me look. That isn't a shot pouch at all."

She pried it out of Ned's mouth and turned it over in her hands. His teeth had torn into the leather which, she now saw, was fitted tight over a lining of tin.

"Mother, what is this?" she asked.

Joanna Spencer sprinkled more sand on a splotch of blood, then looked up. "A water canteen," she said after a moment. "See? It has a drinking hole at the top."

It was empty now. Not a drop came out when Amity turned it upside down. "How would Matt come to have a water canteen?" she asked.

"Likely issued by the Continentals," her mother said. "Our army may not be as badly supplied as we feared."

Amity held the canteen toward the hearthlight. It was scuffed and stained, but she could see that it was made of beautifully tanned leather. There was even a small design tooled in gold on one side.

"How handsome it is," she said as she admired the graceful pattern glinting in the firelight.

Her mother wiped her hands on her apron and took the canteen. "It's fine indeed," she said. "Meant for an officer, I warrant, and not a common soldier. Odd that Matt should have a canteen of such value." She ran her hand over the rich leather and admired the golden design.

"Beautiful," she went on. "A crown, and two flowers."

Amity took the canteen back. "No, not flowers at all," she said. "I think . . . yes, it's letters. See how delicately scrolled they are."

She traced the golden lines with her finger. "One is a 'G' and the other, I think, an 'R.' 'G R.' Might that stand for someone's name?"

For a long moment there was no answer.

"Mother? Mother, what . . . ?"

Joanna Spencer spoke at last, her voice almost a whisper. "A crown," she said. "And . . . the letters 'G R.' I can scarce believe it."

"Believe what?" Amity asked impatiently. "Is it a name?"

"Not a name in the proper sense," her mother said slowly. "The letters stand for the words 'Georgius Rex.'"

"Odd words for certain," Amity said. "What do they mean?"

"They are Latin," her mother said. "They mean . . . 'George the King.'"

Amity jerked her hand away from the canteen. "You mean *King George*? The king of *England*?"

"Aye," Joanna Spencer breathed. "The very king who wars against us."

"Then this . . . why, this belongs to one of the enemy," Amity said. "However would our Matt come to have such a thing?"

She turned to look at Matt, deep asleep on the pallet.

Wake up, Matt! she cried silently. Oh, wake soon!

CHAPTER
9

❖

When he did awake, it was sudden, and with a wild shout. He struggled to rise, but Joanna Spencer leaned close. "All's well, Matt," she soothed. "You're safe here with us."

"Matt, we thought you dead weeks ago!" Amity burst out. "Ben Tyler came and said you'd been killed in a battle. Oh, I'm so glad you're safe! But where have you been?"

Slowly his eyes cleared. "With . . . the army . . . of Burgoyne."

Amity's eyes widened. "Oh, Matt!" she gasped. She held up the canteen. "So that's where you came by this!"

Matt shuddered and turned his head away "No," he said. "It was . . . there is much to tell."

"Best start where it starts, then," Joanna Spencer said, and they both moved close, for his voice was low and hoarse.

"The . . . battle," he said, pushing the words out through his swollen lips. "I was with Ben and the others, lost them in noise and smoke. Shot at anything red that moved. No time to reload. Clubbed them down with my gun—don't know how many. A big one came at me . . . I slammed my gun into his belly. Knocked the wind out of him. Ready to hit him again but . . . a lead ball came past me and . . . and tore his face apart. Then . . ."

He stopped. He's remembering the screams, Amity thought. Like Ben.

"Dead men, dying ones . . . all around me," Matt went on. "Couldn't see through the smoke . . . couldn't breathe. Of a sudden I was off to the side of the field, in thick woods. Got behind a big tree to bring back my breath. Rammed a load of shot into my gun. Thought to get back to General Arnold and the others. But then . . ."

He closed his eyes, blinked them open. "Fearsome noise from the woods behind me."

"What was it?" Amity heard her mother ask.

"Burgoyne's German troops. Hundreds—tall as giants in high metal hats and yellow pigtails down their backs. Running . . . bayonets pointed straight ahead, officers whipping them on like horses."

"Did they see you?" Amity had to know.

"Rolled under the bushes, prayed they wouldn't. Some passed so close I could see the dust on their boots."

He swallowed, and went on. "Then they were on the field, pushing our men to retreat. It was coming on twilight . . . field getting dark. Gunfire dying away. When . . . when the smoke finally cleared, I couldn't see any of our own troops. Gone. All but the dead and wounded left behind . . . and me."

The hearthfire snapped and the baby whimpered in his sleep, but Amity heard only Matt's voice. She felt as if she too were crouched beside the battlefield in the darkening day.

"Were you hurt?" Joanna Spencer asked.

"Not a scratch," he answered.

They stared at the raw red cuts on his face and arms. Blood had begun to seep through the bandage on his leg. Under it was a terrible gash. "Then how—?" Amity began, but Matt's hoarse voice, stronger now, rode over her questions.

"Getting dark fast," he went on. "Watched for a chance to get away, but redcoat sentries were posted at every edge of the field. So . . . I hunkered down in the bushes. Stayed there all night. Never hope to see another night like that."

It was a terrible night he described, full of the cries of the wounded and the sound of shovels digging deadpits. "The British took their own wounded off to hospital tents," he said, "but our men . . . they ran them through with bayonets where they lay. Tossed all the bodies in the deadpits, didn't matter whether they were ours or theirs. After the women took the clothes and boots."

"Women?" Amity's mother was startled. Amity too wasn't sure they had heard aright.

"Aye," Matt said, "women come from England with the army, to be with their men. All over the field they went, with torches and lanterns, pulling clothes off dead soldiers. Every so often there'd be terrible crying and wailing. Must have been when a dead redcoat turned out to be a husband or sweetheart."

Amity was startled to see her mother's eyes mist. Pity for these women? Why, they're enemies same as the soldiers, she thought angrily. Hateful creatures come warring against us along with their menfolk.

For shame, Amity Spencer, she thought in a sudden burst. They are only women who chose to act rather than stay behind and suffer. Not long ago weren't you longing to be a part of things too?

No, these women are enemies, she told herself firmly. Polly would say so too.

She fixed her attention back on Matt. "Watched for hours," he went on. "Hoped when they were done with the dead they'd march back upriver to their big camp at Saratoga. Soon as sunup I'd find my way back to our camp. But they didn't leave. Made camp right there on the battlefield—set up tents on that muddy, bloody ground. Got cookfires going, and lud, didn't my stomach roll when . . . when they wiped blood off their bayonets and slid salt pork on 'em to roast in the fires."

Amity felt her own stomach turn. Still, she had to hear more. "Go on, Matt."

"The Germans set their tents on my side of the field. So close I hardly dared breathe."

"Oh, Matt," Joanna Spencer murmured. "You spent the whole night hiding from the enemy."

"Aye, the whole night. Not sleeping—too cold and hungry, and scared. Morning came up foggy. Prayed the river mist would hold so I could creep off under its cover. But the Germans were swarming all over, putting themselves in order and taking a long while about it. Greased their mustaches with tallow and braided each other's pigtails. God's truth, Amity, they made more fuss with their hair than ever Polly does." The old Matt would have said it with a grin, but this Matt had not the smallest smile in him.

Amity pulled her shawl tight around her shoulders. She

hated these pigtailed German soldiers who hired themselves out to an English king, killing men they had no quarrel with. All for a few coins a day.

"After a while orders came for the Germans. Make foot back to base camp at Saratoga. Luck, I thought, but by the time they were gone the mist was gone too."

Matt moved to sit up, winced, and lay back. "Redcoat sentries all around . . . patrols in the woods. If one stumbled over me, he'd shoot me where I lay. What a sweat I was in, until it came to me . . ." His words stopped while he shifted his leg painfully.

"What came to you?" Amity asked impatiently.

"Small chance of staying alive by hiding under a bush, but if I could make myself one with the army . . . So I crawled away from the bushes, stood myself up, and legged into the camp."

"Into the midst of the enemy!"

"Aye, right up to a redcoat officer I went, and said, 'Please, sir, be this General Burgoyne's army? Where do I go to enlist for a king's soldier?'"

"Wait till Polly hears!" Amity said.

"What then?" her mother asked.

"He drew his sword at me. But I kept on about wanting to join up and shoot me a bunch of those rebel Americans. Told him I'd always been a loyal Tory wanting a chance to help good old King George. Next thing I knew I was writing my name in a muster book. That's all it took. From then on I was part of the army of Gentleman Johnny Burgoyne!"

Matt lay back, spent.

Joanna Spencer looked at him in amazement. "And that's where you've been these weeks?" she asked.

Matt nodded. "Hauling water and digging slop pits for redcoats."

"Oh, Matt!" Amity said in wonder. "Think if you'd been found out!"

"Almost was," Matt said, "the day Cheppa John caught sight of me."

The name stopped her breath. "Cheppa John?" she managed to say. "He was in Burgoyne's camp?"

"Aye, more than once. Came legging in with a backpack, trying to sell trinkets to the soldiers. Must have had finer goods for Gentleman Johnny, for oft I saw him go right into the general's headquarters."

"How odd," Amity heard her mother murmur. She herself had no words, only a warm feeling of thankfulness. He was safe then—peddling, not soldiering. Away from danger.

"What happened when Cheppa John saw you?" Joanna Spencer asked.

"He was that surprised," Matt answered. "'Well, Matt,' says he, 'when last we met you were off to soldier for General Gates. Are you now deserted to the enemy?' I went cold for fear someone would hear and start wondering about me."

"What did you do?"

"Looked him straight on. 'And are you now trading with the enemy?' I said. I thought it might make him angry, but he only laughed."

Amity fancied she could hear Cheppa John laughing. She

knew well how he sounded and looked when amused. "Did he . . . did he say anything?"

"'What harm to sell goods wherever one can?' says he. 'A man of trade is loyal only to his own pocket.' I kept my mouth tight against any more talk, and from then on I made sure to stay out of his eye."

"He was there often, you say?" Amity's mother asked.

"Aye, though it seemed to me a fool waste of time. Not many ribbons and laces can a body sell to soldiers close to starving."

"Starving?" Joanna Spencer said in surprise. "With so many wagons of supplies?"

"Mostly gone," Matt said. "And the countryside just about picked clean of crops and game. Aye, it's a hungry army Gentleman Johnny has now. Powder and shot aplenty, but the men live on scraps of salt pork and moldy biscuits. Close on to two weeks I was there, and never was my belly full from the day I joined in with them. Before I left we were put on half rations, and some of the men were killing baggage horses for food."

"I can scarce believe it," Joanna Spencer said softly.

"It's the truth," Matt said. "Oh, it was a grand force that took Fort Ti, but the army is much smaller now. I heard talk of thousands who died in the wilderness, and six hundred more killed in Freeman's cornfield. With my own eyes I saw men dying of camp fever, and new deadpits being dug every day."

Amity saw her mother lean close to Matt. "Then is Burgoyne's army so weak that he must leave off the invasion and retreat?"

Matt shook his head. "I wish it were so," he said, "but he's in a rage to break through to the river road. The men drill every day, readying a new attack."

"But you said they're starving," Amity said. "And sick."

"Aye," Matt answered, "but they're the king's army, trained to fight. If Burgoyne sets 'em to battle, they'll be soldiers enough. And in truth," he went on, "though they lost many cannons in the wilderness, there's enough left to blow holes in our army. If it comes to another battle, Burgoyne could break right through our lines."

"But we have Morgan's riflemen," Amity said. "Ben Tyler told us about them. He said they're such good shots they never miss."

"Even the best shot can have his head blown off by a cannon-ball," Matt said.

Joanna Spencer looked thoughtful. "Still . . . a much weak-ened army," she mused. Suddenly she stood up.

"Matt," she said, "we must make you fit again quickly. In a few days you'll go to Stillwater, first to your family to let them see you're alive, and then without delay to the Continental camp— not to fight, mind you, but to tell General Gates what you've learned about the enemy's weakness."

"Aye," Matt said. "But I'd sooner tell General Arnold. He's bolder, and—"

Amity had no mind for generals. "Matt," she burst out, "tell us the rest. However did you get away?"

He started to talk, but his face sagged and his voice trailed off.

"Not now, Amity," her mother said. "The boy is spent." She held the bowl of gruel to his lips, and Amity bit back her impa-tience as she watched him drink.

In a few moments he was able to speak again. "From the start I was looking for a way out," he told them. "Kept my gun close and my ears wide to each day's sentry password, but patrols were always in the woods and would as soon shoot a man as a rabbit. Then a morning came when riverfog rolled in thick as a blanket. My chance."

"What did you do?" Amity prompted him.

"Picked up a bucket and headed out of camp, whistling as if I didn't know a care. Gave the password to the sentry and said I'd been sent for water. Soon as I was deep in the woods I just kept on going."

"Did no one see you?" Amity asked. "What of the patrols?"

"I saw *them*," Matt said. "Sweet targets their red uniforms were in the mist, but I was not about to pot one and bring a swarm of others down on me. Crawled past under fog cover till I was well away from the camp. Thought if I took a big circle south and east I'd meet up with patrols from our own camp, and they'd see me back to General Arnold and the others. But . . . a rain came up, and I lost my bearings. Not a track or a trail to guide me, and not a glimmer of sun. Stumbled around all day, and spent the night up in a tree, listening to wolves howl."

Wolves. Tomorrow, when Matt was better, Amity would tell him about the one that had attacked Ned.

"Cursed myself for not having taken even a biscuit to eat. Next day the fog sat so thick I couldn't tell east from west, but I kept going anyway. And then, just before nightfall, I . . . came upon . . . a man."

A shadow passed over Matt's face. His voice faded to silence.

"A redcoat?" Amity prodded.

Matt shook his head. "A man I'd seen around Burgoyne's headquarters. Tall and thin-faced, wearing a brown jacket that hung loose on him. One of Burgoyne's couriers."

Amity remembered what Ben had said about couriers and secret messages. "Did he fight you?" she asked.

Matt closed his eyes, as if to blot out an ugly image. "He was past fighting," he said. "I came on him in a gully, near dead."

"Shot by a patrol," Joanna Spencer said.

"Nay," Matt said slowly. "Attacked by wolves."

Amity gulped down a knot in her throat.

"He'd fallen into the gully and broken a leg," Matt went on. "A pair of wolves had been at him, bad. They were there, shot dead with his pistol, but not before they had right torn him to pieces. Half out of his mind with pain he was, and even though I knew him for Burgoyne's man, I had to do something, so I climbed down. Couldn't do much but give him water from his canteen. . . ."

Amity and her mother exchanged glances.

"It was getting on to nightfall," Matt went on. "Couldn't leave him alone in the night, so I hunkered down next to him. Prayed there'd be no more wolves, but . . . but one came, a big one. Knocked me over with its jump, and started to . . . I grabbed the man's pistol and killed it while it was still . . . still at me."

Amity turned her face away. She had longed to know, but now it was hard to listen.

"No more came," he managed to say, "but all night the woods were full of animal noises, and the man kept crying out strange things that made no sense. Then toward morning he . . . went quiet, and then . . . and then he was dead."

Amity and her mother waited for the cracked voice to go on.

"Scraped him a grave in the floor of the gully. Heaped earth and rocks over him . . . best I could do. Dragged myself out and crept on through the woods. By chance I came upon woodsigns I knew—trail marks I'd made in summer, running a trap line for foxes. Knew then I'd gone in the wrong direction all along. Wasn't anywhere near our camp. Not far from home, though, if I could make it. . . ."

"And you did!" Amity cried.

"Aye," Matt said, "but our house . . . empty. Barely made it up here to you folks, and if you'd been gone too, I don't know what . . ."

Joanna Spencer touched his arm. "You're safe now," she said. "All's well."

"Aye," he agreed, staring into the fire. "But not for that poor soul dead in the woods. Wild and raving he was at the end. Kept shoving his canteen at me and saying, 'Peddler chap—give it to the peddler.' Over and over he said it. Queer, isn't it? I was glad to have a water kit, though, so I took it."

Joanna Spencer frowned. "Peddler chap?" she said. "He must have meant Cheppa John."

"So it's something the man owed him in trade," Amity said.

Her mother's face held its frown. "Why would a dying man think of trading? And what worth would a British canteen be to Cheppa John?"

Ned was chewing on the canteen again. Amity coaxed it

away from him and looked at it curiously. "He could melt the tin down for a saucepot," she said, "and use the leather for . . . oh, Ned—look what you've done!"

On one side the dog's teeth had torn strips of leather away from the tin container. "It's ruined," Amity said. "And it was such beautiful leather. . . . Wait, what's this?"

She held the canteen closer to the hearthlight. Something white was hidden between the leather and the tin. She peeled back shreds of leather and carefully eased out a piece of thin paper crowded with small, ornate writing.

"Whatever can this be?" she asked.

Joanna Spencer reached for the paper. Amity saw her hands tremble as she smoothed it out on her knee. "It's . . . some sort of letter, I think," she said. "At the top it's addressed to someone, and at the bottom—aye, here's a signature."

The name was written large and grand, adorned with scrolls and flourishes. It was the bold, swirling signature of General John Burgoyne.

10

❖

Amity had to strain to hear her mother's voice.

"It is meant for . . ." Joanna Spencer began. She looked up at Amity and Matt, then bent to the paper again. "It says, 'To His Excellency the Most Honourable General Sir William Howe.'"

"Howe? He's the British general who holds New York Town!" Matt cried.

"Oh, quickly—read it!" Amity said. "What does it say?"

Joanna Spencer steadied herself. Then she read:

"My Dear Sir:

I beg your assistance immediately.

I lie at stalemate near a village called Saratoga, facing the army of General Gates encamped north of the town of Stillwater. Two weeks ago this force of rebels gave unexpectedly strong resistance in battle, and although my men held the field, many of them were lost. Now disease and hunger have weakened us even more, and each day our position becomes more perilous.

Without your aid I cannot hope to reach Albany. You

must move your army north on the instant, Sir, and attack the Americans from the rear.

Your move must be immediate, for although we are well supplied with weapons and ammunition, we have but scant food and medicine left.

If by the seventh day of October fortune should have prevented your arrival, I shall have no choice but to mount an attack without your support. On that I day I shall order a full assault with artillery, massed volley, and bayonet, trusting that the surprise and force of such an attack will overwhelm the rabble under General Gates' command and help put an end to this war so foolishly waged by arrogant and rebellious colonials.

Make haste, Sir. I rely on your honour as a soldier and a gentleman, and your loyalty to the King whom we both serve.

Your most humble servant,
John Burgoyne
Commander, His Majesty's Expeditionary Army of the North"

There was no sound but the crackling of the fire.

At last Joanna Spencer put the letter down. "An attack for certain," she said in a near whisper. "And the seventh day of October is but four days away."

"He'll have no help from General Howe," Matt said. "It's good fortune the letter never got through."

"He'll attack nonetheless," Joanna Spencer insisted. "The letter says so. Surprise and force, it says. A full assault."

Amity went tense with fear. Father . . . a surprise attack . . .

But Matt was right. There would be no second army moving to attack from the rear. Good fortune indeed that the courier had not passed the letter on to . . .

No! she cried to herself. It can't be!

Yet here was the truth, lying in her hand. Leather and tin meant to carry more than water. Meant to hide a secret—a secret known only to those who passed it along, from one courier to another, until the letter finally reached General Howe.

Slowly she worked her way through the ugly thought. The canteen was no payment in trade between a man and a peddler. And Cheppa John no longer a mere peddler.

The room spun. Cheppa John a courier for Burgoyne! A . . .

She could hardly find the words. Turncoat. Tory. Enemy spy. It can't be—he wouldn't! Still . . .

"A man of trade is loyal only to his own pocket," he had told Matt. Worse, she could hear his voice, in this very room, arguing with her father.

"There's no standing against Burgoyne . . . let him have Stillwater and get on to Albany . . . all for the best . . . the war is only a foolish row over a tax on tea . . . a king has a right to tax . . ."

And her father, leaning into Cheppa John's face. "That's Tory talk."

They had believed his answer. "I'm for independence," he had said, but it had been a lie.

Amity sprang up, but there was no escape from the feelings that stabbed her.

How foolish I've been, she thought. Not to have read the secret hidden behind his eyes. Not to have known that one who saw so much into other folk and revealed so little of himself would of course be fit to play both sides.

Foolish! More foolish by far than Polly with her light-minded yearning for romantic excitement. Flashing her dimples at Ben Tyler, at the miller's sons, at Captain Dunn, Polly had not not cared a pin for any of them. Not fixed on any special person with . . .

Amity admitted it. With love.

For she had loved more than his way of life. The traveling about to new places, the meeting with new people, the wagon full of laces and ribbons and books—all had been wondrous to think about, but . . .

But what she had truly wanted, she now knew, was simply to be with him. She remembered his hand on hers when he gave her the book. His finger on her lips and cheek, his rain-gray eyes searching hers, telling her without words that she was grown now, no longer a child.

The room was still spinning. She steadied herself against the table. How long had he been playing his double role? When had he made his first contact with the enemy? Why had none of them ever suspected?

None of them, she thought. Least of all myself.

From somewhere far away, voices swam at her, sounding near as stunned as she.

"But this means . . . no, I can scarce believe it," her mother was saying. "Cheppa John is an enemy courier!"

"Now I see," Matt said slowly. "That's why he was in

Burgoyne's headquarters so many times. What a fool I was to think it was peddling that drew him there."

No bigger fool than I, Amity thought miserably.

"He was our friend," Joanna Spencer said in a sad voice. "He and his father . . . such a part of our lives . . ."

Matt was trying to puzzle out something. "Why use two couriers to send one message?" he mused. "Ah, I see it. The river!"

Amity made herself listen. "The river is the fastest way to send a message to New York Town," Matt went on. "But our cannons above Stillwater guard the river so close, not even a muskrat can get past."

Something of the old Matt shone in his eyes. He shifted onto his elbows. "Aye, that would have been the plan. Send one courier overland around both camps, through the woods. Who would question a plain-dressed man out hunting? Once on our own road to Stillwater, he would meet with the second courier."

"And who would question a peddler? Especially Cheppa John," Joanna Spencer said bitterly.

Matt nodded. "Aye. He would hide the canteen among his wares, go to Stillwater, and pass it along to . . . likely to a Tory fisherman. In two days General Howe would have Burgoyne's letter, and troopships would be sailing upriver to surprise our men from the rear."

Joanna Spencer gave herself a shake. "It's of no consequence now," she said in a sharp voice. "What is important is that in just four days Burgoyne will attack. General Gates must have this letter as soon as can be."

She bent over Matt. "You must go early tomorrow, Matt.

You'll ride our Jess, and you need go only as far as Stillwater. Give the letter to your father. He will know how to get it to the Continentals."

She frowned at his bandaged leg. "Will you be able to do it?"

Matt made a try at his old confidence. "Never you fret about me," he said.

"Good. Now, no more talk. Amity, fetch another pillow. We'll bed Matt down for a true sleep."

As they eased the pillow under his leg, Matt gave them a small smile. It was a poor copy of his old grin, but it was a smile nonetheless.

Amity smiled back. "Oh, Matt," she cried. "It's so good you're alive!"

She tossed in bed, for the ugly thoughts came crowding back.

Surely he would not spy for Burgoyne, said a voice in her head.

He is a man of trade, another voice answered. And the British pay in gold, not useless Continental dollars.

But he came to warn us about the invasion.

And would not go with Father and the others to fight.

She felt her hands clench. Half Indian, half French, half Yankee—and now another half after all, a secret Tory half that had turned traitor for British gold.

No! It isn't true! the first voice insisted.

But the other voice was stronger. Why else would he be so welcome in Burgoyne's headquarters? Why else was the dying courier so anxious for him to have the canteen with the secret letter? No, Cheppa John is on Burgoyne's side as surely as if he wore a red uniform.

She felt her mother sink down wearily beside her. Amity reached for her hand. "Another battle," she whispered.

Her mother's arm went tight around her. "But our troops will be forewarned and ready."

It was hard to bring forth the next words. "Cheppa John," she said at last. "Is he truly working for Burgoyne?"

Her mother gave a long, sad sigh. "It seems so," she said.

"I always thought him a Patriot. And a . . . friend."

"So did we all," her mother said. "But war changes people. I pray Matt will reach Stillwater without meeting him on the way."

Amity shivered. Her mother drew the quilt around her shoulders. "Sleep now," she said. "By day's end tomorrow Matt will be with his family again and General Gates will know of Burgoyne's secret plan. All will be well."

Amity burrowed deep under the quilt. All will be well, she repeated to herself.

All except the terrible truth about Cheppa John.

Matt was worse in the morning. He lay twisting in feverish half-sleep. A heap of blood-soaked cloths and the dark smudges under her mother's eyes told of hours spent tending him during the night while Amity slept.

Baby Jonathan was worse too. He squirmed in his cradle and wailed piteously.

"He's all splotched with red!" Amity cried.

Her mother nodded, tight-lipped. "Best get to morning chores," she said in a flat voice.

Amity snatched up the gun and hurried outside with Jonathan's cries still in her ears. Shivering in the October dawn, she raced to the cowshed.

It's but some baby illness, she said to herself. Mother will dose him and he'll mend. But Matt—oh, Matt, be better, be better! The words turned into a chant as she milked Lady and pastured the animals.

Jess looked up when she swung a saddle onto his back. "You and Matt will be journeying today, Jess," she told him. "Carry him swift as you can, for Father's sake . . . and ours."

As she hurried back to the house, the chant came again: Be better, Matt, be better.

She found him awake, but not better. His leg, unbandaged now, was swollen to an ugly purplish red, and his eyes glittered with fever. Now burning, now shivering, he lay exhausted on the pallet.

There was no sitting down to breakfast this morning. Amity took a corncake from the hearth oven and bent her head. Dear Lord, she prayed silently, let Matt soon be fit to take the letter. Please, please, Lord.

The corncake tasted like dust.

Anxiously she and her mother nursed him—cool water for his feverish body, ointments to draw the infection out of his leg, clean wrappings for the oozing wounds. Amity could hardly bear to look. She set foul, bloodstained cloths to soak in the crock, scrubbed others clean and hung them to dry at the hearthfire.

"Bring more, quickly," her mother said, but Amity could find no more, so she scrambled up to the loft for her summer petticoat and tore it into strips.

The baby needed nursing too—poultices on the angry rash that covered his small body, doses of wormwood and sweet basil. Amity and her mother moved from one to the other, silent and tense.

And on the table lay Burgoyne's letter.

October 4 already—what are we to do? Amity asked herself again and again, and this new chant was one of despair, not hope.

Suddenly an answer came, and she straightened up, startled. It was unthinkable. Foolish and frightening. Beyond all doing.

Yet . . . it must be done.

Polly would not hesitate. She could see Polly's red braids bouncing, her eyes sparkling with excitement. Eager, bright-spirited Polly would think it a grand adventure.

But Polly is always bold, never uncertain, she argued with herself. She's made of whole cloth, while I'm a patchwork person—parts of me sure, others full of doubts, and everything stitched together with knots and tangles.

Stop! she ordered herself. Think how you've carried your load and Simon's this long time. How you went after the wolf. And how you've held secrets. Burgoyne's letter will be but one more.

She looked down at the letter. *A full assault,* the elegant writing said. *The surprise and force of such an attack will over-whelm the rabble . . .*

Sudden anger swept over her. We'll see about that, Gentle-man Johnny Burgoyne!

"Mother?" There was something in her voice that made her mother turn and look full at her.

Amity drew a deep breath. "The letter," she said. "I will take it."

11

She had expected a startled "No!" But although her mother's hand went to her throat, her eyes held Amity's for a long, silent moment. She has been thinking this very thing, Amity realized.

"Aye," her mother said at last. "There is no other way."

"You? Amity, you can't!" Matt rasped.

"She must," Joanna Spencer said. "And we must think how it is to be done." There was only the smallest quaver in her voice. She spoke as if planning a day of ordinary chores.

"You will have to stay the night with the Prestons, as Matt's family did," she began.

"The Prestons are Tories!" Matt protested. "Farmer Preston wouldn't join us on the march to Stillwater. He and his sons—aye, his womenfolk too, stood at the roadside jeering."

Joanna Spencer stiffened. "Still, they'll give you shelter," she said to Amity. "Your father helps them each year with their harvest. Mind you say not one word about Matt, or Burgoyne. Or Cheppa John."

"They'll ask why I'm on such a journey," Amity said. "What shall I tell them?"

Before her mother could answer, a loud cry from the cradle sent her rushing to the baby.

Matt struggled up onto one elbow. "Amity, lean close," he said.

She knelt beside him and felt the heat of his fever. "It's true, you must go in my place," he began in a voice thin as a thread. "There's a creek over a plank bridge. Mind that Jess keeps his footing on the planks. You'll know the Prestons' by the red-painted house with two chimneys. When you get to Stillwater . . ."

"Oh, Matt, don't tire yourself," she begged, but he went on.

"Aunt Kate's shop is in her house, hard by the Blue Eagle Inn, on the main street of the town—the river road. Look for a signboard in the shape of a barrel."

Amity remembered what Polly had said about the Widow Becker's shop. She felt a prick of curiosity.

"Give my father the letter as soon as—"

"As soon as I get there," Amity promised, but she could see Isaac Thomas's hollow-cheeked face and hear his deep, wracking cough. "What if he should be too ill to go to the Continental camp?" she asked.

Matt drew a painful breath. "Aunt Kate will know someone who can be trusted. Just put it in her hands, Amity. That's all you need do."

All. The anger that had carried Amity to this moment was fast fading. Fear was creeping into its place.

I cannot do this thing, she said to herself.

You must, her own voice answered. There is no one else.

She straightened up. Best to pretend away the fear. "I'll take a bundle of food," she said, hoping to sound as matter-of-fact as her mother, "and hide the letter inside."

"No!" Matt said. "Anyone on the road may steal it from you."

"In my shoe, then," Amity said quickly.

Matt groaned. "The worst place of all. Have you forgotten Nathan Hale?"

She felt the blood drain from her face. A year ago young Nathan Hale had been caught near New York Town with secret documents in his shoe. He'd been hanged by the neck as a spy, by order of General Howe himself. *And what if I am discovered with the letter?* she wondered with a shudder. *Would Burgoyne hang a sixteen-year-old girl by the neck?*

She glanced around the room to mask her uneasiness. Where could she hide the letter? The canteen was a ruin, and she could think of no other place.

Her mother gave the baby to her. "Hold him while I make a fresh poultice," she said.

Amity took the squirming baby and leaned her cheek against his hot, bobbing head. "Hush, lovekin," she crooned. "We must think of a safe hiding place for . . . oh, Jonathan, don't grab at my buttons. No, don't pull . . ."

Thread snapped. "Oh, bother!" she cried. "Give me the button, sweetling, so I can sew it back on."

She pried the button away from him, and stared at it. Large, round, covered with the same homespun as her dress, it lay in her hand like . . .

Like a hiding place.

"Mother—Matt!" she whispered. "We must cut the letter into pieces!"

At last it was done. She had cut the other three buttons from the bodice of her dress, slit the thread that held the cloth to the wooden forms, and peeled off the circles of wool. Her mother had cut Burgoyne's letter into four pieces, working between the lines of writing. Together they had smoothed each piece over a button mold and pleated the corners down underneath.

"The paper is thin—mind you don't tear it," her mother warned.

It was slow work, but it could not be hurried. Squinting over their stitches, they fitted each circle of cloth over the paper-covered wood and stitched the cloth tightly on the underside. Amity felt her needle tremble. Never had it been so important to make each stitch perfect.

Now, at last, the buttons were sewn back onto the dress. "Stand quiet," her mother said. "Let me look at you."

Amity stood still and held her breath till she saw her mother nod. "Good," Joanna Spencer said. "No one will ever know."

There were no wrinkles, no puckers, no telltale thicknesses. Nothing to show that under the drab circles of wool lay bits of paper that could be pieced together to reveal the enemy's secret plan.

Now there was nothing left to keep her from going. "Are you ready, Amity?" Joanna Spencer said.

Amity nodded, swallowing hard.

"Hold to the main road," Matt said. "Don't go off on any cross-roads or byways."

"I will. I won't," Amity answered.

"Keep Jess to a steady pace," her mother added. "Give him time to rest, and let him drink from roadside streams. And after you have given over the letter, ask Matt's aunt Kate to find someone trustworthy to ride home with you." The instructions had been repeated many times. Now her mother was wrapping the words around her as if they would keep her safe.

Matt raised himself on one elbow. "You'll take to Aunt Kate, Amity," he said. "She's made of strong stuff."

I am too, Amity thought, hoping it was really true.

Her mother drew her into her arms. "Safe journey," she murmured as they clung together. After a moment Joanna Spencer turned away and opened the heavy door.

Amity tightened her shawl around her shoulders. Then, before she could falter, she stepped out into the bright October sun and did not look back.

On the road Jess was willing, but slow. "Hurry, Jess!" she begged. "Please go faster!"

He flicked his ears and obliged with a few swift strides, then settled back to his steady jog. It was the best he could do.

"It's all right," she said with a sigh, as much to comfort herself as him. "I don't mind stumping along like this."

But she did mind. It was miles to Stillwater, and the day was sliding away. Even now Burgoyne's men, ill and starved as they were, would be making ready for battle.

She rode astride, her dress bunched over the old saddle. Long ago her father had traded John the Chapman prime deerskins for the saddle and harness. She remembered how Cheppa John had watched and listened, and how he had smiled at her when the trade had been made.

"Now you're all set to go a-riding, Amity," he had said in his teasing way.

"No, *I'm* to ride Jess!" Simon had burst out. "He told me so himself!" Everyone had laughed, for they all knew of the "talks" Simon had with Jess and the other animals.

"Well, Simon, tell Jess he mustn't forget he's a plowhorse," Father had said with a smile. "The saddle is just in case any one of us might ride him sometime."

For Simon, "sometime" had been almost every day, except during spring plowing or times when Father needed the horse for hauling or loaned him out to a neighbor. Amity had ridden Jess too, but never as much as Simon had. And never as far as she would ride him this day and the next. Jess, like herself, had never been to Stillwater.

He didn't seem to be in a hurry to carry her there now. She tried not to be impatient with his slow, ambling walk.

"Remember how Simon had that special way of making you trot, Jess?" she said to him. "He'd whistle in your ear and you'd go as fast as you could."

She leaned forward and gave what she thought was Simon's whistle, but Jess only twitched his ear as if a fly had settled in it.

"Well, never mind," she said. "We'll get there, you and I." She dared not think what the journey would be like without him.

There was much to avoid thinking about. Matt feverish and in pain, the baby sick, and her mother alone with both of them. Father in another battle against Burgoyne. Cheppa John.

She drew in her breath at the thought of him. He was the enemy now. She must put his name and his face out of her thoughts. Out of her life.

But she could not do it. Even now he might be somewhere near, looking for the man with the canteen. He could not know that the man lay dead in the woods. What if he should come along this very road, searching for him?

The buttons seemed to burn circles into her skin. What would I say to him? she wondered nervously. How could I meet his eyes? Dodge his questions? Above all, keep my own secret and pretend not to know his?

Lies seem to come smoothly to him, she thought bitterly. How could I make them come as easily to me?

Jess snorted and lost his stride as a pair of squirrels chased each other across the road. Amity gripped the reins tighter. Stop your foolishness, she told herself firmly. No one, not even Cheppa John, can think the buttons anything but ordinary. Only the Thomases will get to see the secret under the cloth, and oh! when they do!

She fancied she could see their astonished faces when she told them Matt was alive—Mistress Thomas joyful and rosy again, Isaac Thomas's thin face glowing, and Polly's eyes bright as she laughed.

Amity saw herself laughing too, at last. What relief to have Burgoyne's letter on its way to General Gates, and she on her own way back home. Likely Mistress Thomas would insist on coming back with her, to nurse Matt. They would take up their lives again on their farm, and . . .

And what?

Well, it was foolish to try to look farther. This day and the next were enough.

"Think, Jess," she said, "by this time tomorrow you'll be in the Widow Becker's stable with fresh hay and a bucket of feed, and Matt's father will be off to the Continentals with the letter. Then, when the battle begins, won't Gentleman Johnny himself be the surprised one!"

For a moment her own spirits were high, and she began to take pleasure in the journey. The sun had burned off the last tatters of morning mist and the countryside had come alive. Birds flashed through the bushes, greedy for late berries. Squirrels darted under the trees, rustling through the brown leaves after acorns. Overhead an arrow of Canada geese honked across the sky.

But there is no other sign of life, she realized with growing unease.

Houses were shuttered, and fields were overgrown with weeds or charred black where crops had been burned. There was not a cow or a sheep in sight, not a dog running up to bark. She strained to find a strand of smoke rising from some unseen chimney, but there was nothing but a dreamlike emptiness. In this part of the valley people had heeded Captain Dunn's warning. They had burned their fields and fled.

What if the Prestons have done the same? Amity worried.

And the town folks! What if there is nothing left in Stillwater but empty shops and houses? No Aunt Kate, no Thomases, no way to get the letter to General Gates.

It can't be, she told herself. She tried to bring back the joyful scene she had imagined, but the picture was dim now.

"Shall I sing us a song, Jess?" she said, but her throat was so tight that the song was only a small tuneless croak.

Suddenly Jess lifted his head. Hoofbeats! They were muffled and far away, but coming on swiftly. Amity twisted around, straining to see, but there was no cloud of dust behind, no flash of motion ahead. She swung Jess off the road, scrambled down from his back, and pulled him behind a stand of red sumac. "Not a sound, Jess," she whispered, and tried not to tremble as she stood close to his side.

Two horsemen pounded up the road and swept past, long dark cloaks streaming behind them. There was a flash of scarlet as the wind whipped back the edges of their cloaks.

Redcoats? Had Burgoyne broken through the American lines already? Amity pressed closer to Jess and stood quiet—waiting, listening. There was nothing to see but trees and brush and the strangely empty countryside, nothing to hear but the shrill cry of a crow.

Finally she led Jess out of the bushes. "All's well, Jess," she said, struggling to make her breath come evenly. "Likely they were not Burgoyne's men at all. We mustn't think that every bit of red has a Britisher inside."

She pulled herself up onto his back and twitched the reins to send him forward. Untied her food bundle and tied it again, tighter. Brushed grass off her skirt, picked off burrs. Busy work, meant to keep her hands away from the buttons. It was not easy to keep from fingering them, from thinking about them.

Nothing is going to be easy this day, she realized. But I am bound to it, for there is no other way.

As the day wore on, the sun beat down strong and made the wool dress itchy and hot.

"Look, Jess, there's a pasture with a pond," Amity said. "It's time we had a rest." She slid down from his back and led him through a gap in a low stone wall. While he drank from the pond and grazed, she sat under a tree picked clean of apples and opened her food bundle. She tore off a chunk of bread and bit into the cheese.

How are Mother and Matt? she wondered. And Jonathan? It seemed like days since she had been with them.

She looked over at Jess. Poor Jess, it's a long journey for you, she thought. How much longer do I dare let you graze?

Drumbeats brought her to her feet. She ran to Jess, but it was too late for cover, for she saw them coming and surely they saw her.

It was a company of men with muskets. They marched—no, shuffled, to uneven drumming, and Amity saw that the drummer was a boy younger than herself. At a signal from a tall man in front, they straggled to a halt near the pasture.

They put Amity in mind of Father and the valley men. They had no uniforms, but were dressed in rough towcloth or linsey-woolsey. Men on our own side! she thought with relief, then pulled herself up with caution. It might be a company of Tory loyalists. They had something of trained military bearing to them, ragged as they were.

"Compan-ee, halt!" the tall man called. "This your pa's land, miss? Mind if we use the pond to cool off a bit?"

"N-no," she called back, not knowing which question she was answering.

"Compan-ee, fall out!" the man shouted, but most of them were already scrambling over the stone wall and heading for the pond. Amity stood close to Jess and ran her hand nervously over the buttons, but the men paid her little mind. With shoes and stockings off they waded into the water, splashing and hooting at each other.

The tall man leaned his musket against the tree and pulled out a tobacco pouch. "Name's Captain Fitch," he said. "This here's my militia company, from Briggstown in Pennsylvania Colony."

American militia! Amity felt a flood of relief. "Oh!" she cried. "Are you on your way to General Gates's camp?"

The captain laughed. "No, lass," he said. "We're on our way home from there."

"But you can't be!" Amity cried. "There's going to be . . . I mean, Burgoyne might attack! There might be another battle!"

"Wal, if there is, ol' Granny Gates'll just have to do the best he can without us," Captain Fitch said. "Eh, Jemmy?"

The drummer boy grinned as he climbed out of the water. "Yer right, Cap'n," he answered, and turned to Amity with a gap-toothed grin. "Afore long we'll be back in Pennsy-vanier where we belong."

Amity stared at Captain Fitch. "The war's not over! How can you leave?"

"Easy," he answered with a shrug. "Signed up for two months, and two months is what we gave 'em. Time now to pull foot for home."

"We ain't Regulars, missy," said a short, stocky man. "Them Continentals are regular army, in for a year."

"Aye, poor fools," put in a man with a thick brown beard, "and the Lord help 'em, what with that everlastin' squabblin' goin' on between the gen'rals."

As the men pressed tobacco into their pipes, the short man struck a flint and lit a small greasy cloth from its spark. He held the flame to his pipebowl, then passed the cloth around. "By gravy," he said with a chuckle, "it'd almost be worth stayin' around to see what Gen'ral Arnold is going to do next to rile up ol' Granny."

Ben and Matt had talked about General Arnold, Amity remembered. A great fighter, they both had said. She tried to think how being brave would "rile up" General Gates. And why did they call General Gates by such an odd nickname?

The voice of the brown-bearded man broke into her thoughts. "By gor, that Arnold's a soldier!" he said. "Fought like the very devil himself in that battle, all the while Granny Gates was sittin' at his desk gettin' splinters in his tail."

The men laughed.

"Were you there?" Amity asked.

The man coughed and blew out a puff of smoke. "For a time,"

he said. He brushed tobacco crumbs off his breeches and moved away.

Jemmy grinned. "Caleb ran like a rabbit," he told Amity. "Arnold had the men all fired up to fight, but shucks, Caleb ain't no soldier, no more'n any of us. I seen lots of men skin out."

Amity felt her face tighten. "My father was in that battle, and so were other men from hereabouts, and they didn't skin out."

"They wouldn't, them Yorkers," someone said scornfully. "The fight's on their own land. But there ain't no need us gettin' killed for folk who live up here."

"My father didn't go to fight just for Yorkers," Amity burst out. "He said that if Burgoyne breaks through, the war will be lost. Then the king will take away liberty everywhere, even . . . even in your precious Pennsylvania."

In the awkward silence she could not meet their eyes. Had she really said such a thing? She'd acted as bold as Polly, and as thoughtless.

The short man peered closely at her. "What's a young 'un like you doin' talkin' such sass about the war? Didn't yer ma teach ye to keep yer tongue between yer teeth?"

Amity felt her face flame. "Please," she begged Captain Fitch. "You can't go home now. When Burgoyne attacks, General Gates will need you!"

The captain knocked the ashes out of his pipe. "Burgoyne ain't going to attack," he said. "Any day now he'll pull back to Fort Ti and hunker down for the winter, drinkin' toasts to the king."

Amity fingered the buttons. I'll show them the letter—give

it to them, she thought. Then they'll march back to camp and give it to General Gates, and . . .

She looked at the men lounging on the grass, muttering among themselves. No, she decided. They've set their minds against staying to fight. And they don't look the kind to keep a secret as important as this.

Captain Fitch picked up his musket. "Compan-ee, form ranks!" he shouted. "Stir your stumps, men, we got a mighty lot of marching to do afore sundown."

Amity watched the men straggle back over the wall and gather in ragged formation on the road. At Jess's sudden neigh she spun around. The brown-bearded man was pulling at the harness.

"I could use me a horse," he said. "Even a sorry-lookin' nag like this would be easier than marchin'."

"No!" Amity cried. "You can't have him!"

"Sure I can," the man said as he made to mount Jess. "I'm a soldier, ain't I? Just like your pa."

"Leave the girl's horse be, Caleb," the captain ordered. "If anybody rides, it'll be me. Hand over the reins."

"You can't take him!" Amity cried. "He's old, not even fit for plowing anymore. And he . . . he's lame."

Captain Fitch squinted at her. "Then why is he saddled?" he asked.

"My . . . my little brother likes to sit on him and pretend to ride," Amity babbled. "His name is Simon and he's gone now— in the house, but . . ."

Captain Fitch gave her another searching look, then turned

to Caleb. "Form ranks, I said," he ordered. "Leave the horse alone."

Caleb grunted and tossed the harness straps aside. "A sorry nag," he muttered as he gave Jess's flank a slap and tramped off. Without another word Captain Fitch strode away too.

"Set us a faster pace, Jemmy," he called to the drummer boy. "The sweetest wife in all Pennsylvania is waiting for me."

Amity held tight to Jess's reins as she watched the men shoulder their muskets and move off to the ragged beat of the drum. In a moment they had turned down a byroad and were almost out of sight.

"We'll wait a bit longer, Jess," she said as she patted him. "Can't chance that someone might look back and see us ride off."

At last she led him out of the pasture and swung herself up into the saddle. Her hands were shaking. "Oh, Jess," she whispered. "I need you so."

Then she set her shoulders as she had seen her mother do, and pointed him toward Stillwater.

"That rest did us both good, Jess," she told him as he plodded along. "A few hours more and we'll reach the Prestons' farm. Tory or not, Farmer Preston will have good hay for you, and a warm barn for the night."

On she talked, glad for his company, using words to cover fearful thoughts.

Are there more men leaving the American camp? Will there be enough left to fight Burgoyne's well-trained troops?

And what was it the men had said about General Gates and

General Arnold? That one was brave and one was not? That they were fighting with each other? How can battles be won when generals quarrel among themselves?

Amity shifted uneasily on Jess's back. None of this mattered to the Pennsylvania militiamen. For them the danger was over.

But not for Father.

CHAPTER

12

❖

The westering sun threw long shadows in front of them. Amity twitched with impatience. She remembered how Captain Dunn had galloped so swiftly up to the valley men. A mount like that, she thought, would have put me in Stillwater long before now. Then, remembering how the captain's horse had reared up on its hind legs, she smiled wryly. And long before now I'd have been thrown in the dust, she told herself.

She gave Jess an encouraging pat. "Prestons' farm can't be much farther," she told him. "See? There's the creek, and the plank bridge Matt said to watch for."

Not far beyond the bridge, she saw people straggling down a narrow, rutted wagon trail that crossed the road.

"Whoa, Jess," Amity said softly, and sat quietly on him to watch.

It was a small group, not more than twenty. They trudged along in grim silence. A thin-lipped woman holding a hen under one arm walked beside a man leading an old horse piled with blankets and patchquilts. A crying baby rode in a sling across the back of a woman with a blank, pinched face, and bedraggled children scuffed along, their untied shoe latchets dragging in the dust. Thin, scruffy dogs trotted near the slowly moving wheels of three battered farm wagons loaded with house-hold goods.

Who are these folk? Amity wondered. She had never seen such a caravan.

Bedding spilled over the sides of the wagons. Spinning wheels, tilted at crazy angles, clattered against reed-bottomed chairs, milking stools, churns, and wooden farm tools. Every-thing was piled in heaps, as if whole households had been flung into the wagons. A gaunt, narrow-faced man in ragged homespun sat atop a wagon drawn by an ox. The other wagons were pulled by thin horses that plodded along, heads down, straining against harnesses that dug into their bony necks.

As Amity watched, the shabby little group trailed to a stop at the crossroads.

"We'll rest here for a spell," shouted the man driving the ox. "You young 'uns bring water for the animals."

Grumbling, the older children pulled wooden buckets off the wagons and dragged them toward the creek. They stared when they caught sight of Amity and Jess.

"Ma, here's a girl on a horse!" one of them shouted.

A woman looked up from pounding a stake into the ground beneath an oak tree. "Hey, girl," she called, "bring yourself over here and set a while." She lifted a pig from one of the wagons and tethered it to the stake.

Amity hesitated. She dared not waste time, yet hours had

passed since Jess had had his last rest beside the pond. Silent, lonely hours. Besides, there was something about these people that tugged at her curiosity.

She slid down from Jess and led him slowly forward, making her way around the pig, which was nosing for acorns. The dogs ambled up, sniffed, then lay down in the shade of the wagons, muzzles in the dust.

The woman with the pig eased herself onto the ground and smoothed her stained, tattered skirts. Nearby, the thin-lipped woman with the hen set it down, shouted to a little girl to keep it from straying away, and settled herself on the ground too. Amity sat down beside them, holding Jess's reins loosely as he grazed.

"Where ye be goin' all by yourself?" asked the pig woman.

"To Stillwater," Amity answered, and added carefully, "on an errand for my mother."

"That so?" said the woman. "Well, you and your ma ought to be settin' your feet toward the south. Ain't no place safe around here."

Amity made no answer to that. "Where are you bound for?" she asked.

"As far away from here as we can get," the thin-lipped woman answered. "Sal and me and the others came down from the north settlements. Left our cabins and crops to get away from them redcoat devils. Look what they done to Nance."

She jerked her head in the direction of the woman with the baby. Sitting apart from the others, the woman was nursing the baby and gazing at the ground through long strands of hair falling over her face.

"Lost her husband to a British scouting party," Sal, the pig woman, said in a low voice. "Choppin' stumps in his own field he was, when up come a bunch of redcoats and shot him dead, right on his own land."

"Them devils," said a gray-haired man nearby. He spat on the ground and Amity saw his bony fists clench.

Several children had wandered over and squatted near Amity, staring curiously at her. One little girl clutched a cornhusk doll and looked at Amity with wide blue eyes. Another sucked on a dirty thumb as she fingered a faded red ribbon that held some of her hair out of her face. Close by, the man with the long narrow face leaned against a tree, mending a broken harness strap. His dark, watchful eyes took in the whole group, and Amity wondered if she just imagined that they were resting longer on her and Jess.

In the silence, she felt she should say something. "Have you been traveling long?" she asked politely.

The thin-lipped woman sighed. "Ever since old Noah loaded up his ark, seems like," she said.

"We been two jumps ahead of the British ever since Fort Ti," Sal said, her eyes on the woman with the baby. "It was Nance's husband gettin' killed that decided us."

"Aye," said the gray-haired man—Sal's husband, Amity guessed. "Time to git out when a man can't be safe on his own land."

A wave of unease washed over Amity. It was hard to talk to these ragged, grim-faced people. And the way the women's eyes took in her dress, her shawl, her shoes, the food bundle tied to Jess's saddle . . .

She crossed her shawl over the buttons. "Where are you heading?" she asked once more.

"It don't much matter," Sal's husband answered, "long as Burgoyne's not headin' there too."

"Stillwater might be safe," Amity suggested.

"Naw, not far enough south," said Sal's husband. "Besides, we ain't much for towns. All we know is how to take a livin' out of the land."

"But you could join up with our army and fight," Amity said. "My father did. He's there now, with other men from this valley. There's a whole Patriot army standing against Burgoyne and the king."

The narrow-faced man snorted. "I ain't got no quarrel with ol' George," he said. "Let him king it over me all he wants, long as I ain't got none of his redcoats on my tail." He made a beckoning motion to Sal's husband and the two men moved away, heads together, muttering.

"I saw redcoats!" shrilled a small boy who had edged close to Amity. "They had shiny hats and sharp spears on the ends of their guns."

"I saw the king!" shouted another boy. "All dressed up in a fancy red coat, with a long sword and a white wig! He was on a big horse and—"

"Aw, that weren't no king," said an older child. "That was just their gen'ral."

"You saw Gentleman Johnny Burgoyne!" Amity said.

The thin-lipped woman frowned. "Some fine gentleman," she said. "Lettin' them troops of his run wild over the country-side killin' folks, burnin' houses." With a sniff she pulled herself to her feet and went off after her hen.

Amity got up too. She needed to get away from these people, to feel Jess's comforting back beneath her again. She gathered the reins more closely and turned to Sal, who had heaved herself to her feet.

"I wish you well," Amity said with a polite smile.

"Wishin' ain't what we need," said a voice so close behind her that she jumped. The narrow-faced man yanked the reins out of her hands and tossed them to Sal's husband. "Take 'im, Jud, and git goin'!" he shouted.

"No!" Amity cried, but the man locked her arms behind her in a grip that ground her wrists against each other. "Let me go!" she screamed. She kicked at him, felt the heel of her shoe smash into his shin. Cursing, he threw her to the ground.

"Load up!" he shouted to Sal and the others.

Amity tried to scramble to her feet, but another shove knocked her back to the ground. Her head slammed hard against the road and pain turned everything dark. Dimly she sensed a swirl of people and animals around her.

"Take her shoes," a boy's voice said, and she felt hands tugging. She kicked out blindly, hit something.

"Owww!"

"Leave her be and git up on this wagon, quick!" a woman shouted.

Whips cracked and wheels creaked. Above it all she heard a neigh of panic that sounded like Jess.

Then silence. And, for a long time, nothing. Only a black, roaring emptiness in her head.

When her senses swam back, she sat up. "Jess!" she cried. Somehow she managed to stand and move forward, arms flailing. She stumbled over the ruts, fell, pulled herself to her feet again, tried to run after . . .

After what? There was no sign of the small caravan. No wagons, no dogs, no people.

No Jess.

She crumpled into a heap on the dusty track and sobbed as she had not done since the day Simon died.

After a while she made her way back to the crossroads. Dragged herself to the creek and gulped cool water. Washed the dust from her hands and face. Tried to calm away a fear worse than any she had known before. This was no fear born of fancied noises in the night or images of unknown dangers. It was a cold, dreadful panic.

The sun was well to the west now. She had lost precious time. And she had lost Jess.

Oh, Simon . . .

There was nothing to do but go on, but now she was deeply, grindingly afraid. She had been distressed at the emptiness of the countryside and uneasy with the militiamen, but what she felt now was different.

It was as if threads holding together some last scraps of courage had snapped. For a moment she remembered longing to be an infant, like Jonathan, yet being angry when Mother or Father had called her "child." Now the two parts of her seemed to war inside her head.

What shall I do? the child-Amity asked.

Go on, of course, the grown-Amity answered.

But Jess is gone. I depended on him.

Pfft! Your own feet can carry you as fast as he did.

It wasn't that. He gave me comfort, made me feel safe. And now . . .

And now she had only herself to depend on.

Foolish Amity. It was that way from the beginning. Didn't you know it all along?

Wearily she stood up. Her hand went to the buttons and she began to coax back her courage.

She had lost Jess, but the letter was still safe.

She had lost the rest of her food, but not her shoes, or her shawl. Or, after all, the strength inside her. Fear could damage that strength, but not destroy it.

Set one foot before the other, the grown-Amity commanded. Soon you'll be safe at Farmer Preston's for the night.

She hastened her steps, for twilight was coming fast. Surely the Prestons' farm will show itself beyond the next bend, she told herself. Or the next. Oh, let it be the next, she prayed, but each turning revealed only another empty stretch of road. Then, at last, there it was—the red-painted house, the two chimneys, just as Matt had said. Amity made herself run.

The doors and windows of the house were nailed shut, and the Prestons were gone.

She made her way to the barn and pulled open the door. Empty, but for scuffs of straw and a few scattered tools. She pushed an empty barrel against the door to hold it shut against an intruder.

Huddled in a corner, bedded down in straw, Amity lay shivering through the night. Though her eyes were heavy with sleep, the least leaf rustle or scrape of a branch jerked her full awake. Finally she slept, in spite of the cold, the fear, and the emptiness in her stomach. It was hours past sunup when she woke.

Mistress Preston's kitchen garden had nothing left in it but a few shriveled onions. They tasted so woody she spat them out. She didn't dare take time to root about in the fields for carrots or turnips, and the sight of Farmer Preston's brown cornfield made battle images jump before her eyes.

Burgoyne had set October 7 for his attack—and here it was October 5! This day the letter *must* reach Stillwater.

Yesterday's bruises and the cold, tense night had left her sore and aching, but she made herself go on. She walked at what she imagined had been Jess's pace. Now it didn't seem so slow, and she found it hard to keep going as steadily as he had.

Where is he now? she wondered. Is the narrow-faced man riding him? Has he had enough to eat? To think of Jess turning into one of those dispirited, bony horses pulling the wagons . . .

She pushed away the thought and fixed her attention on the

road. Each step is one bit nearer, she told herself. How many steps to Stillwater?

Lightheaded with hunger, she felt her thoughts jump about. She tried counting her footsteps—one group of ten, then another—but it was hard to keep her mind fixed on the numbers. She knew only that she must not slow her pace or stop, except once in a while to drink from a small roadside stream.

There were many streams, she noticed, and they all seemed to be trickling eastward. Can it be they're feeding the river? she wondered. Then Stillwater can't be far away! She lifted her face, hoping to feel a fresh river breeze, but the air was still, and leaves falling from the trees drifted straight down.

A sudden noise made her jump with alarm. It was a brown quail fluttering up from the brush. The bird twitched awkwardly across the road, dragging one wing as if it were injured. It was all pretend, Amity knew. The bird was trying to divert her from its hidden nest.

Hide your secret well, Mistress Quail, she thought. The way is full of enemies who seem friends. Trust no one, not even me, for my empty stomach would be glad if I could catch you and cook you. She watched the bird flutter away, and sighed. It seemed like weeks since she had eaten.

Now the road dipped into a hollow, and the dusty ruts gave way to marshy ground. Logs had been laid close together to make a short stretch of corduroy road. Amity stepped carefully, afraid of losing her balance and twisting an ankle, but her heart lifted a little. Surely wet ground like this was another sign that the river was not far away. She squinted at the sun, checked her shadow. It was long past midday, but she must be almost there.

Almost there! She tried to picture the town, told herself that of course it would not be deserted, that everything would be just as she imagined it. Even if it were near onto sundown by the time she arrived, the town would be bustling with life. The Widow Becker would be in her shop, selling the last goods of the day, and her customers would start hurrying home before the nightwatchman called curfew. Children would be chasing each other home, wagons would be rumbling along the street. It all seemed so near, and so real, that she could almost hear the wagons.

She did hear them! Wagons, far behind her, coming across the patch of corduroy road! They were hidden from her now, and she from them, by a curve in the road, but they would be upon her soon. Quick—a hiding place!

She darted into the bushes, crouching low, listening.

And her breath stopped as suddenly as if she had been struck. It was only one wagon, a harness-jingling, wheel-clattering, tin-rattling wagon.

Cheppa John.

CHAPTER

13

Amity froze. Hiding was hopeless. From his high wagon seat he could see over every rock, every clump of brush, every stone wall. And he would be doing that, searching for the man with the canteen. What then if he found her instead, cowering in the bushes like a guilty child?

"What are *you* doing here? Tell me!" he would demand. His eyes would probe at her, his questions would peel back layers of explanations until . . .

Until she babbled out the truth?

No! I can play your game, peddler. Even better than you, for I know your secret but you don't know mine.

So there would be no hiding. Like the quail, she would put herself in the open and pretend. As the sounds of the wagon came closer, she stepped out of the bushes.

The wagon came in sight around the curve. She drew a long, ragged breath.

Now! Waving her arms and shouting, she ran toward the wagon. "Oh, Cheppa John!" she cried out. "How glad I am to see you!"

Toby reared in surprise, nostrils flaring. Tin pots and pewter jugs jangled against each other in great clanking chords. Cheppa John struggled to rein in Toby and stop the wagon.

"By heaven!" he cried. "Amity!" For once there was only one emotion in his eyes. He was astonished, and nothing else.

The questions began as he jumped down from the wagon. "Why so far from home? Are you alone? What in thunder are you doing here?"

"Mother sent me," she said.

"Sent you alone on this road? All this way?"

She gave him a mite of the truth. "The baby is ailing with a fever and a rash, and . . . and there were foragers. We chased them off, but . . . now we're alone, with no one around for miles, so . . . Mother sent me to . . . to find someone in Stillwater to come out and stay with us."

He gripped her shoulders. Once she would have thrilled to his touch. Now she tried not to shrink away. "Foragers?" he said with a frown. "Was it a man? Did your mother shoot him?"

"There were several," she said quickly. "Men and women both." Sal and the others leaped into her mind. "Ragged folk they were, and they ran when Mother shot at them, but . . . they took Jess."

She squirmed away from his grip. It was hard to lie while looking at him.

"There are many such people about," he said, and Amity thought she heard relief in his voice. "But I can scarce believe your mother would send you on such a journey. It is unlike her to admit to needing help."

Amity forced herself to meet his eyes. "At night," she said, "I hear her weeping."

His face seemed to soften. "Aye, it's a hard burden for her," he said, and for a moment he was Cheppa John, their trusted, helpful friend. If only Burgoyne's gold had not turned him into their enemy.

Now he looked at her more closely. She stood stone-still as his gaze traveled over the dusty dress, the mobcap askew on tumbled hair. Amity fought to keep her hands away from the buttons. The sun lay hot on her shoulders, but she crossed her shawl over the front of her dress, as if she needed warmth.

"You carry no food," he said. "Your mother gave you nothing for the journey?"

"I . . . I met a lad named Jemmy," she said. "He was hungry. I gave him the last of what I had."

"Aye, that would be like you," he muttered. "Well then, you'll ride to Stillwater with me. And when you're there, what then?"

This part of the tale was easy, for it was truth. "I'm to go to the Widow Becker's," she said. "The Thomases are there."

He looked away from her. "They'll be pleased to see you," he said. "Mistress Thomas grieves for Matt, and Isaac is doing poorly."

Amity bit her lip. He had seen the Thomases in Stillwater— yet he had not told them Matt was alive! He had never let on that he had seen him well and uninjured in Burgoyne's camp. Why?

Had he wanted to spare them the shame of thinking Matt a turncoat? No, Amity told herself, likely he had not wanted it known that he too had been in the enemy camp. But to let Matt's family go on grieving just to hide his own dealings with Burgoyne . . .

"Spying is a dirty business," Ben had said. And a cruel one too, she thought bitterly.

Well, soon enough she herself would be giving the Thomases the joyful news about Matt. Burgoyne's letter would be safe in American hands. Then let Cheppa John puzzle out who was turncoat and who was true.

Suddenly he jerked away. "Curse those dogs," he said abruptly. "They'll tear their throats out with that barking." He strode to the back of the wagon and climbed up over the tailstep.

Dogs?

Yes, now she was aware of shrill, high-pitched barking. Curious, she followed Cheppa John and looked up into the wagon. Inside, he was pushing aside large cloth-covered bundles, and she saw that there *were* dogs—two of them, small and sturdy, with short legs that scrabbled at the sides of the wagon as they barked.

Cheppa John unsnapped a chain and thrust one of the dogs down at her. "Hold this one," he said. "Mind he doesn't get loose."

Startled, she cradled the dog and crooned to him. He quieted finally, and as his tail thumped against her and his tongue licked her face, she felt a sense of quiet too. It was the first time she had felt calm since Jess had been torn from her.

How Simon would like you, she thought as she stroked the dog. But whatever in the world are you doing with Cheppa John?

He brought out the other dog now, snapped his chain back to his collar, and set him down. "Hold this fast," he said as he handed Amity the chain and fastened the other to the dog in her arms. "Now, let them both run."

Amity watched the dogs skitter to the ends of their chains and scratch in the leaves. Now that she could see them clearly, she thought them odd-looking, with their heavily muscled bodies and short legs. How different they were from Ned and the other large, long-legged farm dogs she knew. Unlike farm dogs, they were frisky and nervous. They sprang about as if wild to run and jump.

It was impossible to hold back delight. "What lively puppies!" she cried.

"No puppies these," said Cheppa John as he watched them closely. "Full-grown dogs they are, and each one worth twelve gold pieces."

Amity gasped. Did people pay such large sums for mere dogs? True, they were lovable little creatures, romping with each other, then scampering up to nip at her skirt and beg for attention. She bent down to pat them. "What are their names?" she asked.

"They haven't any," Cheppa John said, and for the first time he smiled at her in the old way. "If they were yours, what would you call them?"

She looked carefully at the little dogs. They were the same in size and build, but different in their markings. One was darker tan, with white front paws, while the other had a white-tipped tail and a fluff of white on his chest. As they tumbled about, they reminded her of the crisp autumn leaves that blew in the wind.

"If they were mine," she decided, "I'd call this one Chip, and the one with the white on his tail would be Twig."

Cheppa John nodded. "Fitly named," he said, "although their new owner will have no need to call them by name once they're set to work."

"Work?"

"Aye, they're not meant for pets," he answered. "They're bred and trained to be turnspit dogs."

Seeing her puzzlement, he went on. "Turnspitting's a long, tiresome task, is it not?"

"It's hateful," she agreed.

"Well," he went on, "some folks will have their turnspitting done for them by dogs."

Amity glanced at the small, frolicking dogs. "How?"

"Hitch a dog to a special contraption—a treadmill, it's called—and set him to running, and he'll roast you a whole ox without your even putting a hand to the spit. It's a custom much favored in England."

"A cruel custom!" Amity cried. "Who would put poor little dogs to such a thing?"

Cheppa John stiffened. "Many a rich man would be mighty pleased to have this pair," he said. "They are promised, though. There's an innkeeper been waiting a long time for 'em."

"Likely a Tory!" Amity burst out. "Only a king's man would carry on an English custom like that!"

Her face flamed and she turned away. There, she had done

it—lost control, forgotten that he himself had turned into a king's man. To cover her distress she made a show of brushing mud from her dress.

Cheppa John gave a short laugh. "I don't guess a man's feelings about the king matter so long as he's willing to pay good gold," he said. "Peddling is a business."

So is spying, Amity wanted to retort. She bent to pat one of the dogs, not daring to look at Cheppa John. How rich the war is making you, she thought. Burgoyne pays you "good gold" to pass along secret messages, and innkeepers open their purses for slavey dogs. And all the while my father, who trusted you, is . . .

She struggled for control. It was dangerous to let feelings ride over caution.

Cheppa John reached for one of the dogs. "Back they go into the wagon," he said. "You first, Master Chip."

As he climbed onto the wagon's tailstep and chained the dog inside, Amity scooped Twig into her arms. "Let this one stay with me. Please?"

It would feel good to have something to hold, to keep her calm.

Cheppa John frowned down at her. At last he said, "Mind you hold him fast, then. Remember his worth to me."

Amity settled herself on the wagon seat with Twig on her lap and soon they were on their way, rattling over the rutted road. Well, Amity Spencer, she said to herself, here you are where you wanted to be, doing what you longed to do—traveling the countryside with Cheppa John.

But oh, how different it all was. The countryside was deserted. And Cheppa John was no longer the person she had trusted and loved. He was a traitor, and her enemy.

"Too much time gone," Cheppa John muttered. "Faster, Toby." He flicked the reins over Toby's back and set him to a jouncing trot.

Amity did not speak. She stroked the dog, glad for the comfort of him. Poor little dogs, spending their lives chained to a turnspit. No wonder they had been so rompish when Cheppa John released them. She pictured Twig running free in the pasture with Ned, and smiled a little to think of it.

How strange it felt to smile, even for that small moment. For half of forever, it seemed, her mouth had been drawn down by fear.

Take care, she warned herself. The danger is far from over.

He was staring at her again. "You look like a starveling," he said. "It was foolish to share your food with that Jemmy person. What was he to you?"

"Nothing," she said. "Just someone I came upon. I thought it wouldn't matter, since I was close to sheltering the night at the Prestons' farm, but then . . ."

How much should I tell him? she wondered, then decided to go on. "Their farm was deserted. It seemed strange they would leave and run away, I mean their being Tory and all. . . ."

She stopped, horrified. Another slip.

Something flickered in his eyes. "You seem well informed about Tories," he said. "How do you come to know Farmer Preston's loyalties?"

"I ... the talk is ... everyone in the valley says the Prestons are Tories," she blurted out.

"Do they?" he said, and Amity heard a familiar wry note in his voice. "Then it strikes me odd that everyone did not say that the Prestons were run off their land by a mob of their Patriot neighbors."

Amity gasped. "Run off? By Patriots? I thought ..."

He gave her a half-smile. "You thought this war was being fought only by armies," he said. "That all Patriots are good people and all Tories are bad. I tell you, Amity, the Prestons were good people. Their only crime was to remain loyal to the king, and their mistake was to let others know about it."

"What ... where did they go?" Amity asked in a small voice.

"Likely to Canada," Cheppa John answered. "They'll be safe there from 'good Americans.'"

She searched for something to say, but could find nothing. To hide her confusion she bent over and stroked Twig. Sal and the others running away from the "redcoat devils," Farmer Preston and his family fleeing their own neighbors. Was there any sense in what was happening?

"Oh, Amity," she heard him say with a small sigh. "Best keep your thoughts away from such matters as Tories. War is no business for girls."

Or for peddler lads, she answered in her heart. How different everything would have been if the war had not set us on opposite sides.

His eyes were still on her. She turned aside as much as she dared, the buttons burning on her chest like hearth embers.

CHAPTER

14

❖

After a moment she had herself in hand. "It was foolish to give away my food," she said, turning back to him. "Truly I *am* hungry."

A flush spread under his tanned face. "And I am at fault to leave you so," he said. Rummaging in a canvas pouch, he came up with a small loaf. "I've nothing like your mother's good eatings to offer you—just this stump of bread."

He watched her devour the bread, then reached into a sack under his feet and brought out two apples. "Here, Toby won't mind sharing with you."

They were poor apples, dry and shriveled, but Amity ate them down to the cores. She could have eaten the whole sackful.

With a boldness that surprised her, she said, "Have you water? A . . . canteen, mayhap?"

He shot her a frown. "Nay," he said, "no canteen of water." Then, recovering quickly, his face relaxed into a teasing smile. "Nor cider, nor toddy, nor turnip wine. I wager, though, you'll find plenty at the Widow Becker's to slake your thirst."

She shrank back against the seat, her heart pounding. Foolish to have baited him with talk of the canteen. Best watch her tongue more carefully.

Cheppa John had gone silent again, and there seemed a new nervousness in him. She noticed how his eyes constantly searched the roadside, how he tensed each time they came to a deserted farm or an empty byroad.

Suddenly he spoke. "Likely it was a lonely journey for you till I came along," he said. "Unless . . . did you happen upon any other person on the road?"

She decided on a truthful answer. "I met a militia company," she told him. "Their enlistment was up and they were heading back to Pennsylvania."

"Were they now? Aye, the ranks are full of such scarecrow soldiers, ready to turn tail and run at sight of an enemy whisker. Did they talk much about things at the camp? The bad blood between Gates and Arnold?"

Amity shifted uncomfortably. "They said . . . there is a bit of arguing, I think," she answered.

"A bit? They rage all over headquarters, those two, calling each other 'coward' and 'hothead' and worse. The rest of the officers take sides behind one or the other."

How much of this have you passed along to Burgoyne? she wondered.

As evenly as she could she asked, "Why do generals fight with each other when they are against the same enemy?"

His answer was not swift in coming. "An army's a strange collection of men thrown together," he said at last. "Horatio Gates and Benedict Arnold—now there's a bad brew, bound for jealousy and mislike."

"Why?"

"Arnold is a restless man. He was a Connecticut shopkeeper before the war, but you'd think he was born on a battlefield. Happy only when he's on the attack, riding that prancing horse of his and dodging musket balls. Why, even with a leg gone lame from fighting the British elsewhere, he has more fire and spirit than anyone else in the whole Continental Army."

Amity looked up at him in surprise. Clearly he admired this General Arnold. How then could he conspire against him? Burgoyne must pay well.

"Now Granny Gates," he went on, "is slow and cautious, just the opposite of Arnold. Dig the troops in behind barricades, he says, wait and starve out the enemy. Wait until Burgoyne turns his army around and creeps away without a fight."

"But he's wrong! Burgoyne won't do that!" Amity burst out, then felt her face go scarlet.

He turned to her with a look that made her heart jump. "The militiamen said so," she lied quickly. "They said . . . oh, I can't remember it all."

It seemed to satisfy him. "Aye, Gates and Arnold," he said after a moment. "So blind with jealousy that Gentleman Johnny could dance a jig under their noses and they'd not take notice."

That must be what Burgoyne is counting on, Amity realized. Even sick, hungry troops could defeat an army torn apart by its own leaders. Oh, these generals *must* have the letter, and quickly. Once they learn about the attack, they'll put aside their quarrel and stand against the enemy together.

She moved impatiently against the wooden backboard, and Twig stirred sleepily on her lap. How much longer will this journey be? she wondered.

"Is it much farther to Stillwater?" she asked.

The wagon had climbed slowly up a rise. "Look down there," he said as they crested the bluff.

Amity leaned forward. There below lay the town, spread snugly along the edge of the river and framed in a glowing brocade of autumn foliage. It's not burned and deserted at all! she thought with excitement. Which of the houses is Aunt Kate's?

"We're there!" she cried.

"Nigh on," he answered. "A seemly sight, isn't it?"

"Oh, much more than seemly!" With the setting sun casting red streaks across the sky and the river a broad sparkling ribbon, Amity thought it the most beautiful sight she had ever seen.

Now that Stillwater was in view, Cheppa John's face lost its grim look. He thinks the courier must have made his way to Stillwater, Amity told herself. He'll be looking to meet him there at some appointed place. That must be the reason for his change of spirit.

He had even begun to whistle a lively tune over and over. It was a melody she had not heard before, but she liked it, and with a new sense of ease she let herself hum along.

"Ah, you fancy my music," he said, and it was the old, teasing Cheppa John speaking.

"I do indeed," she answered in the old, smiling Amity way. "Is it a new fiddle tune from Albany?"

He laughed. "Not a Yankee song at all," he said. "It's the hit of the London stage, and would you like to guess who wrote it? Gentleman Johnny Burgoyne himself! Aye, before he turned to soldiering. He calls it 'The World Turned Upside Down.'" With that he started to sing:

"If ponies rode men and if grass ate cows,
And cats should be chased into holes by the mouse,
If summer were spring and the other way 'round,
Then all the world would be upside down."

She couldn't help laughing.

"Like it?" he asked. "Here's another.

"Old Goody Bull and her daughter fell out,
They squabbled and wrangled and made a great rout,
But the cause of the quarrel remains to be told,
Then lend both your ears, and a tale I'll unfold."

Amity sat stone-still as he sang on. Lend both your ears? Better to close them and lock them tight. This song seemed to be about a silly family quarrel, but as the verses went on, all she could think about was the real and dangerous one between the American generals.

And about how she had come to Stillwater at last, sitting beside the man with whom she had once hoped to spend her life.

Under cover of stroking Twig, she slanted a glance at him. He was staring straight ahead now, intent on guiding Toby down the winding road to the town below. Nothing about him looked different—not the fringed buckskin tunic and breeches, not the high-boned face and the gray, shadowed eyes. He seemed the same Cheppa John whose hand had closed over hers, whose eyes had sent her silent messages all those weeks ago. She felt the old pull toward him, and with it a sharp pinch of loss and regret.

Burgoyne's own spy he was, singing Burgoyne's own songs. And she, sitting beside him, must pretend that nothing had changed—that she had no notion of his turncoat actions, that she still cared for him as a friend and some-day lover. She felt a deep, wrenching ache inside as part of her longed for him and another part could scarce wait till she was safely gone from him.

Oh, what an upside-down world indeed.

Stillwater had been rightly named. There were rapids upstream, but here the Hudson River was a smooth sheet of water.

Amity felt her weariness melt away. As the wagon lurched down the road from the river bluffs, her excitement grew. She hugged Twig and buried her face in his fur.

"Almost journey's end," she whispered, and smiled when he licked her face.

Twilight came on quickly as the sun dropped below the bluffs. When they gained the river road, Amity saw that many of the houses were indeed deserted, with doors nailed shut and weeds choking their gardens. At other houses, though, candles glowed behind small windowpanes, throwing yellow patches of light into the dusk. Amity peered excitedly over Twig's head. There was so much to see, to hear, to smell.

The river slapped against dock pilings, and a fishy, weedy odor rose from the water. Large gray-and-white birds wheeled overhead, squawking as they rode the warm air currents rising off the land. Amity watched a pair swoop down and bob on the water.

"What birds are those?" she cried.

"River gulls," Cheppa John said. "Hold tight to that dog."

She clutched Twig and squinted into the gathering darkness, straining to take in everything. The wagon rattled past shops shuttered for the night—an apothecary, a leatherworks with a saddle-shaped sign swinging over its doorframe, a cobbler shop marked by a large, brightly painted shoe. There were few people on the streets, but town noises were all around—a dog barking somewhere off in a dim lane, small children's sleepy, whining cries, the slam of heavy wooden doors, the distant clang of the town watchman's bell.

How different it all was from the quiet, lonely farm.

They were nearing a blacksmith's forge now. Amity could see the smith, a large man in a leather apron, banking the fire for the night. He looked up as they passed, his face lit red by the glowing embers.

"You're late, peddler," he called cheerfully. "Curfew's begun. Mind the watchman doesn't clap you in jail."

Cheppa John answered with a wave, but kept Toby to the same plodding pace. Amity longed to put Twig aside, to jump down from the wagon and run the rest of the way. Surely she could find Aunt Kate's house herself. Hard by the inn, Matt had said, with a sign in the shape of a barrel.

No, she told herself, pretend calmness this small bit longer. Wait till Cheppa John draws up in front of the house, then hand the dog to him, step down, and make a polite thank-you. Off he'll go then, and let him search the whole town for the courier. This day he has ridden next to quite a different one!

It was hard to sit still. She hoped Cheppa John would take her fidgets for excitement at being in the town. Faster, Toby, faster! she urged silently.

As if he had heard, the horse quickened his pace. "Toby smells the end of the journey," Cheppa John said. "Look there."

It was the inn, fronting on a broad cobbled courtyard lit by pine knots ablaze in iron baskets. An American eagle spread blue-painted wings on a signboard swinging from a pole. Black letters proclaimed:

BLUE EAGLE INN
THADDEUS GREENE, PROP.

Horses hitched to a wooden rail at one side of the courtyard whickered, and men's voices rumbled through the open top of the Dutch door. Amity paid no mind. She leaned forward and peered into the darkening street. Which of the nearby houses was Aunt Kate's? Where was the barrel-shaped sign?

To her dismay Cheppa John turned Toby into the innyard. "Cheppa John!" she cried. "I must go to the Widow Becker's!"

"I'm afraid that will have to wait," he said. "First I have business here." The wagon clattered around to the side of the inn and drew up in the shadow of a large stable.

"Zeb Greene!" Cheppa John shouted. "Come stable my horse!"

There was no answer. "Lazy lout," Cheppa John muttered as he climbed down. "Heaven help anyone cursed with a son like that. Here, give me the dog."

Amity gave Twig a last hug and handed him down. It was sad to think of him once more chained in the back of the wagon, but she could not make it her concern.

"Zeb Greene!" Cheppa John shouted again, and Amity wondered why he had suddenly grown so snappish. Whoever you are, Zeb Greene, come quickly, she prayed silently. Let Cheppa John set about his business so I can slip away and find Aunt Kate's house.

Would he be surprised to find her gone? Not likely, she decided. He seemed so bent on his business here that he might even be grateful she had gone off by herself.

She could hear him rummaging in the back of the wagon. "Wait here," he called to her. "Mind you keep watch while I fetch the innkeeper's clodpate of a son."

Wait here? With the Thomas family so near? With secrets bursting inside her? Indeed not. She gathered her skirts to climb down, then stopped in surprise. Cheppa John was hurrying toward the inn, carrying both dogs.

A side door opened at his knock. Light streamed out, and with it a smell of roasting meat that made Amity's stomach twist with hunger. "Ho, peddler!" she heard a voice shout. "So you have brought my little slaveys at last!"

So this was the innkeeper with the "good gold" to buy dogs for his turnspit. Let him not pay too quickly, she prayed. It was dark now, and she would need time to find her way across the innyard, lit only with patches of flickering light.

"Stand quiet, Toby," she said, hoping he would understand. She put a foot over the side of the wagon.

But suddenly Cheppa John came striding back. Beside him shuffled a sour-looking, thickset lad of about sixteen. Amity could hear him grumble as they drew near.

". . . like a common stable boy," he muttered. "My father—"

"Your father set you this task," Cheppa John reminded him. "Now help me unload this contraption."

Amity shrank back unnoticed as the boy followed Cheppa John to the back of the wagon. This must be Zeb Greene, she thought—the innkeeper's son. She wondered why he had Cheppa John's dislike. And such a dislike. This was a side of the peddler she had never seen.

She peered around the side of the wagon and watched them unload an odd assortment of iron rods, cranks, and pulleys. As the last of the pieces of iron clanked onto the ground, Cheppa John straightened up. "That's the lot," he said. "Now bring a bucket of water for Toby and haul these to the kitchen."

"You've no cause to order me about," the boy fumed.

Cheppa John laughed. "Ah, Zeb," he said, "you'd have plenty

of ordering about if you were off a-soldiering like others your age. Here now—give me that!"

Amity saw him take a flat, cloth-wrapped bundle from the boy. "This is for me alone to put into your father's hands."

Still grumbling, Zeb shouldered a few rods and shuffled off, brushing past his father, who had come hurrying out of the inn. Thaddeus Greene was portly, with a round, flabby face and brown hair tied back in a club. He puffed up to the back of the wagon, his eyes on the pieces of metal still on the ground.

"It's all here? Everything? Good, good." As he rubbed his hands nervously against his leather apron, Amity saw the glitter of a large gold ring. "The signboard too?" he asked.

Cheppa John's voice was businesslike and brisk. "All here, just as you ordered," he said. "Three guineas for the sign, twelve for the dogs and wheel. Hard money, mind you—no Continental dollars."

"Yes, yes, I know our agreement," the innkeeper retorted. "But the dogs . . . it will be five guineas now and the rest in a week, after I have seen them work to my pleasure."

As the bargaining went on, Amity hunched on the wagon seat. Chill river dampness had begun to creep into her, and she missed Twig's warmth. She longed to be gone from this place.

"The dogs are of no value to me if they don't work well," the innkeeper said.

Amity wondered at the anger in Cheppa John's voice as he replied. How different he was from the respectful young man who bartered with her father!

"Six guineas now and not a penny more till next week," Master Greene said.

"So be it," Cheppa John said at last, and Amity heard coins clink from one hand to another.

"Now let me see the sign," the innkeeper said. As the men moved into a patch of light cast by the burning pine knots, Amity could see the innkeeper's smug smile and the anger on Cheppa John's face.

Zeb Greene was back, with a leather bucket of water. He slung the bucket over Toby's nose and cursed when the water splashed his knit stockings. A small sound from Amity made him glance up.

"Who the devil might *you* be?" he growled. "Why do ye stare at me so?"

But she was not staring at Zeb. She was looking past him at his father, who had loosened the cloth covering the flat bundle and was holding a wooden board up to the flickering light. It was a new inn sign. Gold lettering spelled out:

RED LION INN

THADDEUS GREENE, PROP.

Under the letters pranced the proud British lion, splendid with bright red paint and a glittering golden crown.

Master Greene ran his fingers over the lion. "Good, good," he said with a smile. "Well, peddler, if all goes well it won't be long till my true colors can be seen. I'll have this up the minute Burgoyne routs those Yankee plowpushers and starts down the river road. Ah, and when Gentleman Johnny gets here, I'll bring out the fine Jamaican rum I've been saving for him."

Cheppa John gave a short laugh. "Burgoyne has no need of your rum," he said. "His men have dragged wagonloads of French wine through the wilderness for his pleasure. And though the army starves, his cooks still set him a fine table."

What curious game is Cheppa John playing? Amity wondered. He deals with this Tory innkeeper and keeps his secret, yet seems to dislike him mightily.

The innkeeper looked uncomfortable. "When will Burgoyne make his move?" he asked in a low voice.

Amity held her breath.

"I know not," Cheppa John said, "and it is not a matter to speak of here." In a few steps he was back at the wagon, reaching a hand up to Amity, smiling at her. "Now then, Amity, down with you."

"What's this?" demanded the innkeeper. "Who might this girl be? How long has she—"

"She's been here all this time, Pa," broke in Zeb Greene. "I saw her. She heard everything you said."

"Peddler!" stormed the innkeeper. "I demand—"

"Have done," Cheppa John snapped. "She's but a farm lass I found on the road. And by the look of her she's too worn down with weariness to know what any of this babble is about. Come along, Amity."

Stiff with cold, Amity stumbled after him. She was glad to be taking leave of this Tory innkeeper and his whining, sour-faced son. Would she feel the same when Cheppa John parted from her at the Widow Becker's?

They were in the front courtyard of the inn when Cheppa John turned back for a last word.

"Innkeeper," he called, "see you save a bed for me—one without too many fleas. And you, Zeb—bed Toby down in the stable and stow away the wagon. Mind you, I've a count of everything in it. Let there not be one thing missing when I come back."

"Pa!" whined the boy. "Tell him—"

His words were cut off as the front door of the inn burst open and three men came out, talking loudly. As they strode to the waiting horses, Amity saw the flash of brass buttons on dark blue coats with buff facings. Continental Army officers!

Cheppa John grasped her arm and drew her into the shadow of a tall hemlock hedge. She saw Thaddeus Greene quickly put the signboard facedown on the cobblestones. He bustled forward to the men, rubbing his plump hands together.

"I do hope you gentlemen enjoyed the Blue Eagle as usual," he said in a soapy voice. "It is always a pleasure to serve you."

His smile swept all three of the men, but he made a great show of holding the stirrup for one—a short, broad-shouldered man who had limped over to a big bay stallion.

"Do return soon, sir," the innkeeper said as the man swung himself up onto the horse. "That is, ah . . . if your duties permit." There was a smirk in his voice.

The man had a hawk-nosed face lit by flashing blue eyes, and even with the limp he had moved with restless energy. Now he looked down at Thaddeus Greene with a scowl, as if the man's words had stung.

"My duties are light these days, innkeeper," he said. "No doubt we will be back tomorrow to sample your hospitality again."

He tossed the innkeeper a coin and wheeled his horse around in a swift, smooth motion. The riders clattered over the cobblestones in a blur of gleaming boots, bright brass buttons, and red sashes. Their horses' hooves struck sparks on the stones. In an instant they were on the road to the north, swallowed by the darkness.

"Blasted rebels!" Zeb Greene muttered.

Cheppa John stepped out of the shadows and picked up the signboard. "A near thing, innkeeper," he said as he wiped his sleeve over the red lion. "It would not do to have American officers find their host a Tory after all."

Thaddeus Greene snatched the signboard and shoved it at his son. "Take this to the stable and hide it well," he ordered.

Zeb slung the sign under one arm and led Toby and the wagon into the stable, but Amity paid no heed. Her mind was fixed on the dark, brooding face of the man with the limp.

"Cheppa John, that man . . ." she began, and stopped, not knowing how to ask. But the question was in her voice, and his answer, when it came, sent a tremor through her.

"Aye," he said. "That was General Benedict Arnold."

CHAPTER
15

❖

Cheppa John took her hand as they made their way out of the innyard. "It's easy to stumble in the dark," he said.

Amity hardly noticed his touch. Her head throbbed with the echo of the hoofbeats. To have been that close to General Arnold! If only . . .

No, it would have been impossible to approach him, she told herself. A general would give no attention to a young girl. And how could I have given him the buttons with Cheppa John so near?

But the general will be at the inn again tomorrow! Then Matt's father need not ride to the Continental camp at all. She pictured Isaac Thomas going to the inn, drawing General Arnold aside, giving him the pieced-together letter, mayhap right under the nose of that smug Tory innkeeper. Oh, to be there to see it all!

"Mind your step," Cheppa John warned as she missed her footing. He pulled her close to him, and for an instant it seemed as if he would hold her there without moving. It was hard to draw away, but she forced herself to think only of the reasons she had come to Stillwater—to give the Thomases the secret letter and tell them the wonderful news that Matt was alive.

"There's the Widow Becker's!" she said, pulling away to point.

They had come across the road to a large two-storied house set back on a short brick walkway. In the center of the house were two doors, close beside each other, with a large bay window on the far side of each. Above one window, shuttered and dark, swung a signboard in the shape of a barrel. Amity made out the lettering:

EDWARD BECKER

GOODS

Through the shutters of the other window came slivers of warm yellow light.

A surge of excitement drove out her weariness. What matter if she could hardly go another step, if hunger ground deep in her stomach? She was here at last!

Cheppa John clacked the brass door knocker. There was a stir inside. Then a woman's voice asked cautiously, "Who is there?"

"Young John the Chapman," he called out. "And Amity Spencer with me."

The inner bolt slid back and the door was pulled open by a gray-haired woman with a pockmarked face. She peered at them over the light of a candle in a silver holder, but before she could speak, Mistress Thomas came elbowing past with a cry.

"Amity! How come you to be here? Oh, dear child!"

Amity felt herself drawn into a tight hug, heard Polly rush to the door with a happy shout. Then all was a wondrous muddle. Squashed into Mistress Thomas's embrace, Amity could hardly breathe, but it didn't matter. Polly had flung herself at her too, hurling a swarm of questions and not waiting for answers. All was noise and happy confusion, just as she had pictured it, except that with Cheppa John just a step away she could not cry out the news about Matt.

Matt is alive, alive! The words shouted inside her, but she dared not let them out.

The gray-haired woman who, Amity judged, must be Aunt Kate, moved them all out of the doorway. "Come in, come in," she said with a smile. "You also, peddler—do come in."

No! Send him away, Amity wanted to shout. I have news— Matt is alive! But it was no use. Aunt Kate drew both of them into a warm, elegantly furnished room where firelight gleamed on polished furniture and candles glowed in brass wall sconces.

Amity looked for Isaac Thomas. There he was, leaning out of the depths of a large wing chair by the fireside. He struggled to speak, but his words were lost in a fit of coughing, and he sank back into the chair. She was startled to see how hollow-eyed and gaunt he was, how his clothes hung scarecrow-loose on him.

Why, he has become an old, old man, she thought. How cruel to hold back the truth about Matt even for a moment. But she could not tell it now, not even in a whisper.

Mistress Thomas hurried to him and held a linen cloth to his mouth while he coughed. As Amity looked away, she noticed someone else in the room—a small, prim woman in a blue silk dress and lacy mobcap. She sat near a candle stand, working a piece of dainty embroidery. Her delicate fingers, jabbing the needle in and out, reminded Amity of birds pecking at seeds.

"This is Mistress Fassett, our neighbor," said Aunt Kate, presenting Amity and Cheppa John. Amity felt the woman's cold, curious eyes travel every inch of her. She was glad when Mistress Fassett gave her a quick, cold nod and turned to Cheppa John.

"You are travel worn, peddler," she said with a sniff.

"As always, ma'am," Cheppa John said, making a small bow. "I daresay a town gentleman would be also, if he had gone the miles I have these past days."

Amity did not know what to make of this prim, unsmiling woman who turned her head away as if from a barnyard smell. She seemed so different from Mistress Thomas and Aunt Kate. A neighbor, Aunt Kate had said. Another secret Tory like the innkeeper? Stillwater might be aswarm with them, just as Albany was.

Isaac Thomas's coughing spell subsided and attention now turned full on Amity.

"Dear child, sit down right here," Mistress Thomas said as she drew Amity to a silk-cushioned settee. "Now tell us what brings you here. Cheppa John, you are a dear friend to bring her all this way."

He's no friend at all, Amity wanted to say. He's a spy for the enemy, and worse. For weeks he has known Matt is alive, but to protect himself he has not said a word to you.

Polly plumped herself down next to Amity. "How cold your

hands are, Amity," she said. "Let me rub them. Now tell us everything!"

If only I could, Amity thought. Oh, to shout out the wondrous truth about Matt!

But it would have to wait until Cheppa John took himself back to the inn and this prunefaced neighbor returned to her own house.

She struggled to remember what she had hastily made up to tell Cheppa John. Careful not to look at him, she picked her way through the tale. She chose her words with care and hoped they were the right ones.

Mistress Thomas listened carefully, her face puckered with concern. "For a fact, child," she said, "I wish your mother had come along with you. This is no time for her to be out there alone with an ailing babe."

"Indeed," Aunt Kate agreed. She smiled kindly at Amity. "There is overmuch space in this big house," she said. "You and your mother could be comfortable and safe here with us until things settle more. Peddler, perhaps you could go tomorrow and fetch Mistress Spencer."

"Oh, no!" Amity cried.

She felt her cheeks burn under their stares. "Mother can't . . . she won't leave," she stammered. "There's Lady and the sheep, and . . . and your sheep too, Mistress Thomas. She promised my father . . . oh, I know she won't leave!"

She laced her fingers together on her lap and clamped her lips shut. Hunger and weariness were muddling her thoughts. Her flimsy lies had brought a quizzical look to Cheppa John's face, and she felt a new surge of anger against him. Go back to your Tory friends at the inn, she raged silently.

Aunt Kate broke the uncomfortable silence. "Nothing need be decided tonight," she said, and turned to Mistress Thomas. "Come, sister, here is a lass worn out from a long journey, and near faint from hunger from the look of her. What's needed now is warm food and a soft bed."

"Bless me, 'tis so," Mistress Thomas said. "Polly, lay the small table near the window and we'll see to some eatings. You'll stay, Cheppa John?"

"Aye, and with thanks," he said. "I'd much prefer it to the fare at the inn." To Amity's dismay he settled himself in a chair.

She struggled to her feet. "Please, Mistress Thomas, do let me come with you," she begged. "I can help, and . . ."

But Mistress Thomas pressed her back onto the settee. "Sakes, child, you're cold as a stone," she said. "Now you stay right here by the fire."

"But I want . . . I must . . . oh, Mistress Becker, please!" Amity protested.

"Tush, now," said the Widow Becker with a smile. "You must call me Aunt Kate as Polly does. And you must not move from this fireside. It won't be a minute till we fetch some good hot soup to put an end to your shivering."

It was no use. Amity dared not make a further fuss. How much longer? she wondered miserably. She felt choked by her secrets.

Mistress Fassett snipped off a piece of bright silk thread. "And where might your father be, young lady?" she asked.

"With . . . with the Patriot army, ma'am," Amity managed to say. "Fighting against Burgoyne."

"Oh, this dreary war," Mistress Fassett said with a delicate sigh. "I wish your father no harm, mind you, but our scattertail army has faint chance against Gentleman Johnny. It would be far better to throw ourselves on his mercy and bid him welcome to Stillwater like ladies and gentlemen. I only hope he delays until I finish my new rose brocade gown."

Cheppa John gave a short cough. "Beware, milady," he said. "That begins to sound like Tory talk."

Mistress Fassett drew herself up. "I am no Tory, sir," she said. "I'm as good a Patriot as any, but everyone knows we have little chance of stopping Burgoyne."

"Nonetheless," Cheppa John answered, "with words like that you may find yourself dressed one day in tar, not brocade."

Polly, flinging a cloth over the table, began a cascade of words.

"Oh, Amity, you can't imagine the things that happen here in town! Why, I saw a mob drag a man out of his house and cover him with hot tar. I was helping Aunt Kate in the shop and we heard a terrible screaming and we rushed out to see. The poor man! Of course he was a Tory and deserved punishment, but to have buckets of tar poured on him—imagine!"

"Hush your babble, Polly," Aunt Kate said as she set down two bowls of thick soup. Mistress Thomas followed with bread and Indian pudding. "Gracious, child, you needn't sit so stiff," she said when Amity was seated at the table. "You look as if you were among enemies instead of your dear, dear friends."

Amity tried to return her smile. She spooned up some soup

164

and kept her eyes away from Cheppa John, sitting so close to her across the small table.

Isaac Thomas spoke for the first time. "Peddler," he rasped, "do you think Gates can stop Burgoyne?"

Cheppa John carefully tore a piece of bread in two before he answered. "Only if he unleashes Arnold," he replied at last.

"Is Arnold still here?" Mistress Thomas asked in surprise. "Someone said—I think it was the cobbler, no, it was his wife— well, someone told me Gates had ordered Arnold away from camp."

"I heard he refuses to go," Mistress Fassett put in. "Fancy an officer not obeying orders from his superior. Such an unsol- dierly army. No wonder Burgoyne has called us a rabble in arms."

"Best hold your tongue, Amelia," said Aunt Kate crisply. "There's an ugly mood in the town against such talk."

Mistress Fassett twitched her shoulders. "Well, I simply do not understand why we must throw off English courtesy in order to be done with English rule," she said. "The way peo- ple went at poor Tom Wakefield with that tar—why, it was shameful."

Isaac Thomas spoke again, and this time his weak voice shook with anger. "Tarring's no more than a man deserves if he speaks against this country while others die for it."

The room went silent. Mistress Thomas's face puckered. She held her apron to her face, and Amity saw her shoulders shake. Polly and Aunt Kate went to her, and for a moment they all clung together without a word.

Amity looked full at Cheppa John. Tell them Matt didn't die

in the battle, she challenged him silently. Tell them you saw him with your own eyes, alive and safe.

But Cheppa John bent to his food, and she could read nothing in his face.

Mistress Fassett gave an exaggerated sigh. "We never should have begun this war," she said. "It was useless from the start."

Polly patted her mother's shoulder and stepped away. Now, behind Mistress Fassett's back, she was the old comic Polly again, drawing her eyebrows up and her mouth down in a prissy face, holding her homespun skirts out to the side as she dropped a mock curtsy. Once Amity would have laughed at such antics, but not now. She longed to shut her ears against Mistress Fassett's foolish talk. Tory or Patriot, the woman was empty-headed and vain, with no mind for others' sorrow.

Aunt Kate sat down and took up her own needlework. "Arnold is a fierce leader," she said. "Gates may be glad of him if Burgoyne attacks again. Do you think there will be another battle, Cheppa John?"

"Some think Burgoyne may risk such a move," he said slowly.

"What do *you* think?" Aunt Kate pressed.

Cheppa John shrugged. "What can a mere peddler know of battles?" he said. "War has its strategies that only generals know about. Ah, ladies, this is fine fare indeed for hungry travelers."

How well you play the part of Patriot, Amity thought bitterly.

Aware of the part she herself must play, even now, she fought the weight that had begun to press on her eyes. Stay alert, she told herself.

But it was hard not to yield to the warm food and the comfort of this lovely room with its soft furniture and patterned carpets. The miserable night in the Prestons' barn made her ache for sleep.

Polly was chattering again.

". . . and, Amity, wait till you see Stillwater by day. So many people! Not just townspeople either. I heard someone in Aunt Kate's shop say there might be spies all around. And couriers carrying secret messages. Just think of it!"

A sudden dizziness surged through Amity. Through a mist she heard Cheppa John laugh. "Spies, you say? And couriers? Is Gentleman Johnny sending secret messages to his wigmaker?"

"Cheppa John, don't jest," Polly said. "Didn't you hear about the man with the message hidden in the silver bullet? Why, he might have passed right through this very town and no one even suspected. Isn't it exciting! I wonder who else . . . Why, Amity, what's wrong? You're pale as a shade!"

"I . . . it's just that I'm so weary," Amity managed to say.

"Of course you are," Mistress Thomas soothed. "Finish your food, child, and we'll see you into bed."

It took all of Amity's will not to look at Cheppa John, not to clutch her arms tight across her chest over the buttons. She forced down a spoonful of Indian pudding.

"Please, no more talk of spies," Mistress Fassett said with a delicate shudder. "It makes me feel quite ill. Polly, why don't you show your friend the embroidery I've been teaching you?"

Polly rolled her eyes. "Mistress Fassett would turn me into a town miss," she said to Amity.

"Every young lady should work a sampler," Mistress Fassett said with a sniff.

"And every grown woman should milk a cow," Polly muttered.

Mistress Thomas frowned. "For shame, Polly," she said. "Being a town miss is what you wanted."

"Not so I could spend hours stitching letters onto cloth," Polly grumbled.

She went to a nearby drawer and pulled out a crumpled piece of linen. "Here it is," she said.

The sampler was covered with awkward stitches and knotted threads. "I'm not very good at it," Polly said. "And I hate the verse."

"What does it say?" Amity asked. Her eyes were so heavy with sleep that even when she looked close she could scarce make out the uneven lines of letters inside their crooked border of flowers.

Mistress Fassett answered. "It's a verse I worked myself when I was a child," she said primly. "I thought it suitable for these unfortunate times." She twitched the cloth away from Polly and read:

"Declare your secret thought to none,
For fear of shame and sorrow.
For he that is your friend today
May be your foe tomorrow."

Amity pushed away from the table and stood up shakily. "Please," she said to Mistress Thomas, "I need . . . I would like to . . . go to bed now."

She made her good nights in a small voice, sliding her eyes past Cheppa John's. Then, with Mistress Thomas's arm around her shoulders, she left the room, her thoughts whirling.

I'll tell her about Matt as soon as we're alone. . . . No, what if she cries out? She will, I know she will. She'll be sure to run right in to tell the others. Then Cheppa John will know too, and . . .

Oh, what shall I do?

First thing tomorrow, then—dayrise. The letter too.

But oh, these dear, sorrowing people—if only they could know that Matt is alive and safe!

Her head was heavy on her shoulders and she swayed as Mistress Thomas guided her down a hall to the back of the house. Her feet stumbled on the doorstep of a firelit room. An iron kettle hung over the hearth and there seemed to be fragrant herbs somewhere. She bumped into something—a table? Her eyes were too heavy to see clearly. Mistress Thomas took a tighter grip on her and led her around the table.

"Poor tired child," she heard her say. "We should have given you up to bed long ago."

Another doorsill, another room, this one with a large bed and . . . and flowers on the wall? How strange.

She let herself be pushed gently onto the bed. A feather mattress welcomed every part of her, and she sank deep into it. She barely felt Mistress Thomas untie her shoe latchets and draw off her torn, muddy stockings. There was a calm hand on her forehead, and soothing words that were too far away to make out.

"Matt," she heard her own voice say. "I must . . . tell . . ." She fought to blink her eyes open, to drag words past a tongue that would not move.

What words? she wondered foggily. There was something that had to be told, but what was it?

"Hush, child," she heard the faraway voice murmur. "No more talk now. Hushhhh."

Then there was nothing but softness, warmth, and sleep.

CHAPTER

16

❖

The sun, slanting across her face, woke her.

Amity sat up in alarm. There were bright patches of sunlight on flowered wallpaper, and outside the window, gulls wheeled and shrieked over the river.

Long past dayrise—and October 6 already. So much time gone!

She saw she was wearing only her shift, and looked wildly around the room for her dress. With a rush of relief she saw it hanging on a peg beside a washstand. Someone had brushed away yesterday's mudstains and had laid a fresh set of knitted stockings nearby.

Amity scrambled down from the bed. She held her breath until she could feel the buttons, still firmly stitched to the bodice. Still safe. She struggled into the dress, pulled on the stockings she guessed were Polly's, and gave herself silent commands.

Find the Thomases and Aunt Kate, tell them straight off about Matt. Explain about the buttons, undo the cloth, piece together the letter, tell them what must be done. Matt's father was weak, so he would be slow about delivering the letter, but he

171

would do it this day. He had to, for tomorrow Burgoyne would attack!

She went through the cooking room with its bundles of sweet-scented herbs hanging from ceiling beams. Such a wondrous house, but so silent. Where was everyone?

There was no one in the hall. The sitting room, where they had all been gathered last night, was empty and cold, with only dead gray ashes in the hearth. But now she heard footsteps overhead, and voices, underlined by Isaac Thomas's deep cough.

Amity ran to the stairs. She was about to start up when a man in dark brown waistcoat and breeches hurried down past her and went out the door. A moment later Polly came out of an upstairs room, her face twisted as if she were trying not to cry.

Amity ran up the stairs toward her. "Polly, what's wrong?"

Polly launched a tumble of words. "Oh, Amity, Pa is ailing bad this morning. Aunt Kate has been giving him purges and possets since long before sunup, and Dr. Mott was just here to bleed him, but he's already coughed up so much blood I don't know how taking more from him can help."

Her eyes spilled over with tears. "This is the worst spell he's had. I've never seen Mother so set with worry, not since we came here, all of us grieving so for poor Matt. . . ."

Amity gripped her friend's hands tightly in her own. "Polly, listen to me," she said. "Hush now, and listen. I have something wonderful to tell you!"

Moments later a beaming Polly pulled her into the sickroom, and Amity felt feather-light with relief. She had said nothing about the courier or the letter, for Polly's joyful outcries had cut off her words, but no matter. It could wait a few moments more. For now, it was enough for them to know that Matt was alive.

In the darkened room Mistress Thomas's shrieks of joy echoed Polly's. She swept Amity into one of her tight hugs, crying, laughing, full of questions and not waiting for answers. "To think he is safe—and in your dear mother's care!" she said through her tears. "Oh, child, what happy, happy news!"

Amity felt herself being pushed toward the bed. "Isaac, listen!" Mistress Thomas said. "Amity has brought us the most wondrous news—our Matt is alive!"

"Pa!" Polly burst in. "Amity says he hid in the woods the whole night after the battle, and then went right into Burgoyne's camp and made them believe he was a Tory come to join up! Think of it—our Matt! He was there for days, Amity says, and everyone took him to be loyal to the king, and . . . oh, Pa! Matt is not killed after all!"

Isaac Thomas lay in bed like a dry husk, eyes glazed with fever, too weak to speak. Amity looked down at him and felt a stone settle on her.

She tried to smile. "Aye, Master Thomas, Matt is alive," she said. "Weak and feverish from an injury to his leg—that's why he couldn't come here himself—but Mother says he'll heal with time."

As she spoke, careful not to upset him with details of the ugly wounds, she felt the buttons press heavy against her. They were a burden she could not pass on to him.

"Oh, my brave lad," Mistress Thomas sighed. "Think, Isaac, we'll soon have our Matt home with us again."

Aunt Kate's voice broke in quietly. "Amity, how is it you said nothing of this last night?"

Amity searched for words. Was this the time to tell them about Cheppa John? "It seemed . . . I thought . . ." she stammered, "I tried to tell you, but . . ."

"Indeed you did, but we all babbled on so," Mistress Thomas said, patting Amity's hand. "And then, when I took you off to bed, I swear you were asleep on your very feet. All the while Polly and I cleaned your clothes, there was never a sound from you."

Polly grinned. "I can't imagine what you did to your dress," she said. "It looked as if you rolled in mud all the way to Stillwater! What a sight you were last night!"

"And still pale this morning," Mistress Thomas said, peering at her. "Dear child, we must give you food to start the day, lest you fall over in a heap."

"I'll see to it," Aunt Kate said. "Come along, Amity. No, Polly, you stay and help your mother."

Amity gave the sick man another glance, then followed Aunt Kate down the stairs. She knows there's something, she thought with relief. It will be easy to tell her. Aunt Kate is the very one— not Mistress Thomas, busy nursing a sick husband, and surely not Polly, who can't keep a secret beyond her next breath.

Yes, she would put her trust in this strong, sensible woman who was so like her own mother.

In the cooking room Aunt Kate's eyes looked at her steadily.

"Now then, where has Matt been these past weeks? There is more to tell, is there not?"

"Oh, Aunt Kate, there is much more!" Amity cried. And looking into the pleasant, pockmarked face, she began. Now that the words were freed, they flew about like wind-tossed leaves.

"Matt saw Cheppa John in Burgoyne's camp—they even talked! Cheppa John said he was just selling trinkets to the soldiers, but Matt saw him welcomed into Burgoyne's very headquarters."

She hurried past Aunt Kate's startled look. "Aunt Kate, Cheppa John is a spy for the enemy!"

Aunt Kate drew a quick breath. "Surely not!" she said. "Why, I have seen him grow up—and traded with him these three years since his father died. I know him for a Patriot."

Miserably Amity shook her head. "He has tricked us all," she said. "After Matt escaped from the camp, he came upon a man in the woods, dying, and it turned out he was one of Burgoyne's couriers, and he spoke of Cheppa John. Before he died, he told Matt to give—"

Polly rushed into the kitchen. "Aunt Kate! Come quickly!" she cried. "Pa's coughing blood worse than before. Hurry!"

Even as Polly's words tumbled out, a tap sounded on the kitchen door. "Mistress Becker?" a child's voice called. "Are you not opening the shop today?"

Aunt Kate hurried to the door and opened it. A small boy peered up at her, holding a jug. "Ma sent me for m'lasses," he said.

Aunt Kate rubbed a hand across her eyes. "Bless me, is it so late already?" she said. "Yes, of course the shop will open,

William. Go around to the front and we'll see you get your molasses right off."

To Polly she said, "Open the shop, Polly, and do your best till I can get there. It may be a long while."

Polly looked startled. "Alone? Oh, I can't . . ."

"You must," Aunt Kate said. "Folks need their supplies. Come now, you've watched me enough to know what to do. Here, take the keys."

"Sister!" Mistress Thomas's voice called. "Come quick!"

Snatching up a pile of cloths and a tin basin, Aunt Kate whirled out of the room.

Amity ran after her. "Wait!" she cried. "I must tell you the rest! It's important!"

But Aunt Kate had not even a glance for her. "Later, child," she said. She rushed up the stairs and was gone.

Amity stood frozen. Numbly she saw Polly unlock a door next to the stairs. "Amity?" Polly said, looking back at her. "Come into the shop with me."

But she could not make her feet follow. It was all gone wrong. Everything was coming apart, like yarn pulled out of an ill-knitted stocking. Yesterday she had been so sure her task would be done if only she reached this house. Now yesterday seemed a time of foolish imagining.

How right that they call me "child," she thought bitterly. I have been thinking like one, waiting to give this burden over to others.

Something in her mind spoke quietly to her. There is no one to depend on, it said. Only yourself.

176

But . . .

"Amity, please!" Polly called from inside the shop. "I need help."

Amity bit her lip. Not as much as I do, she thought. How can I get the letter to General Arnold?

Without knowing, she had put her hands on the buttons. She could feel Burgoyne's words pushing through the cloth. *Full assault . . . surprise and force . . . the seventh day of October . . .*

Tomorrow.

She straightened her shoulders. I've come this far without mishap, she said to herself. If there is a way, I'll find it.

"I'm coming, Polly," she called, and stepped through the doorway into the shop.

Polly had opened the shutters and was dipping molasses out of a large crock into the boy's jug. He laid a copper coin on the long wooden counter, then made for the front door.

"Take care, William," Polly called after him. "If you spill, your mother will take a switch to you."

She dropped the coin into a box and turned to Amity with a small smile. "Mistress Polly Thomas, shopkeeper. Oh, Amity, it's so lovely to have you here. And to think you brought us such wonderful news about Matt! If only Pa wasn't so sick . . ."

Amity took her hand. "I know," she said, and for a moment thought about sharing the secret. Only for a moment, though, for Polly pulled away, shaking her red braids as if to rid herself of dark thoughts.

"Now heed me, child," she said in imitation of Aunt Kate. "Since you're Polly's helper today, you'll need to know what's in the shop. So take a good look around. Go on." She grinned a bit of the old Polly grin and gave Amity a little push.

There was nothing for it, so Amity wandered around the shop, pretending to be interested in casks of meal and barrels filled with salted river fish. Aunt Kate sold more than foodstuff, she noticed, and many things were strange to her—boxes of snuff, cloth so fine that she could almost see through it, and, on an out-of-the-way shelf, a large tucked bonnet half as big as a washtub.

Time's passing, she told herself as she stared, only half-seeing, at the silky blue folds of the bonnet. What am I to do?

Polly came up beside her. "Watch," Polly said. "It does tricks." She pressed down on the top of the bonnet and it folded flat. "That's so you can store it away easily when you're not wearing it."

Polly snapped the bonnet open again and put it on over her white cap. She pursed her lips and wrinkled her nose in a mimic of Mistress Fassett.

"Oh," she said in a high, prim voice, "I wish this were a different color. It just won't do with my rose brocade gown, and I must look my best when Gentleman Johnny comes to town."

In spite of herself Amity smiled at the sight of the freckled face and red braids peering out from beneath the huge bonnet.

"I do think it's a disgrace," Polly went on in her Mistress Fassett voice, "the way English ships these days can't spare a mite of room for the latest London fashions. Why does the king send us so many soldiers, when it's bonnets we need? Upon my soul, this is such a dreary war!"

Suddenly her face crumpled and her eyes filled with tears. "Oh, Amity," she wailed as she flung the bonnet aside, "do you think my father is sick enough to die?"

For a moment Amity forgot her own predicament and put her arms around Polly. She longed to comfort her, to say no, of course he'd be well again, but no words would come. The ashen face of Isaac Thomas stood in the way.

After a moment Polly wiped her eyes on her apron.

"There," she said with a little shake. "It won't help to carry on like this, will it? It's much better to laugh and be silly. Now tell me more about Matt. Oh, how I wish I'd had some of his adventures. Not the battle, mind you, but just think of being right in the midst of Burgoyne's camp! Did he see Gentleman Johnny? Is he as fine-looking as everyone says?"

As Polly rambled on, Amity turned aside. It had been foolish to think of telling Polly about the letter. A skittertongue is not one to hold a secret. If only Polly were different . . .

But Polly was Polly, and always would be. The task must be seen through, Amity told herself, and one of my ragbag selves must do it. A strange feeling settled over her. For the first time, she was no longer afraid of being afraid.

She could feel her wits working again. She drifted over to the bay window and looked up and down the street. "Polly," she said idly, "do any of our soldiers come into the shop?"

"Some," Polly answered. "But when they're in town it's mostly the inn that gets their trade. Why?"

179

Amity slid over the question and glanced at the inn across the street. "The Blue Eagle," she said. "Have you ever gone there?"

"No," Polly said with a pout, "and I'm not ever likely to. Aunt Kate says it's not a place for females. Think how rowdy it must be!"

"I wish I might go there," Amity said, and added quickly, "Now that I've seen a town house and a town shop, I'd like to see what an inn is like."

"So would I," Polly said with a sigh, "but it's only for men."

Amity frowned. She'd been in that very innyard last night when General Arnold had told the innkeeper he'd be back today. But what chance did she have of going back there herself and giving him the letter if the place was only for men?

Well then, she told herself, I must find a man to act for me. Surely there must be someone.

"Is the Widow Becker not here to serve me?" a testy voice said.

"Good morning, Master Wells," Polly said, bustling behind the counter. "A pennyworth of snuff? Of course."

Amity looked carefully at the thin, gray-haired man leaning on a cane. Patriot or Tory? she wondered. She could not tell.

Other customers came, but it was impossible to judge anyone's true feelings. The saddlemaker, the cobbler, the apothecary—they all seemed like honest townsmen while buying goods in the shop, but any one of them might be a secret Tory like the innkeeper. In her mind she saw the words on Polly's sampler:

. . . he that is your friend today
May be your foe tomorrow.

The morning's slipping by! she thought in a panic, and felt her hopes begin to sag. Will Arnold come to the inn after all? she wondered. Will anyone come from the Continental camp? And what if they do? Trapped here in the shop, I might as well be across the ocean as across the street.

"A cheese, Mistress Taylor?" Polly was saying to a woman at the counter. "Oh, this is the last one. Amity, please go down to the cooling cellar and bring up more cheese. You'll find a tub of it somewhere."

Amity made her way slowly down a flight of stone steps. The cooling cellar lay partly below the level of the river. It was cold and damp, and its stone walls oozed water. In the dim light she could see the dark shapes of barrels and crates, and at last she found the round cheeses. She gathered up an armful, and as she made her way back up the stone steps she was startled to hear men's voices, loud and hearty. Pausing on the top step, she looked into the shop. There, milling about and seeming to fill the whole room, were tall, husky men dressed in buckskin. Each one wore a fur cap and carried a gun as tall as himself.

Amity's spirits swooped upward. Morgan's riflemen! Her chance had come at last!

CHAPTER
17

❖

They filled the shop with their talking and laughing. They were lean and sinewy, leather-faced, smelling of woodsmoke, gunpowder, and bear grease. In their fringed, sweat-stained buckskins and raccoon-tailed caps, they looked strong enough to take on any kind of enemy, even the king's best army.

Amity loved them.

She dumped the cheese into an empty tub and hurried to help Polly measure tobacco onto oiled paper squares.

"Take yer time, little gal," one of the men drawled as her trembling fingers spilled tobacco shreds. "We got the whole day ahead of us, don't we, Hannery?"

"Sure do," answered the man next to him. "Ain't no red squirrel around here."

He winked at Amity. "That's what Dave and me call them fancy Britishers," he explained. "Purtiest targets you ever did see." The men slapped each other's shoulders and laughed.

Amity looked up at them as they stood at the counter, their rifle butts resting on the floor. Make talk, she told herself. Hold them here and find a chance to pass along the letter.

"You . . . must be good shots," she said.

"Oh, middlin'," Hannery answered with a grin. "Tim Murphy here—he's the best in the whole company. Picked off four majors and a bunch of colonels at the battle of Freeman's farm."

The man named Murphy patted his rifle. "Easy as flickin' tails off jaybirds," he said.

"Yessir," Hannery went on, "ol' Tim, he just set up there in a tree and laid them Britishers out like a red rug. Gentleman Johnny didn't like it one bit!"

"Caint blame him," another man said with mock concern. "The king's officers ain't supposed to git shot at."

"Yeah," joined in another, "it ain't civilized. Tim, didn't yer ma teach you no manners?"

The men hooted with laughter. Some paid for their tobacco and waved noisy good-byes. As they made their way out of the shop, their heads barely cleared the doorframe.

Amity cut another square of oiled paper and stole a glance at the three men still at the counter—Hannery, Dave, and the man named Tim Murphy. Do it now, she told herself. Tell them about the letter, snip off the buttons, spread the pieces of writing on the counter. They'll stare in surprise, of course, and so will Polly, but no matter about her till later. The riflemen will race back to camp with the letter. They'll give it to Morgan, and he'll rush it to General Gates, and then—

She came out of her imaginings with a jolt when Hannery tossed some copper coins onto the counter. "Now, lads, over to the tavern!" he said. "Let's get that fat landlord to brew us up some killdevil."

"Oh, wait—stay!" Amity cried.

Ignoring Polly's startled look, she dashed around the end of the counter. "Wait!" she cried again, and clutched Hannery's sleeve.

He looked down at her kindly. "Can't buy nothin' more, little miss," he said. "If ever the Congress pays us for our soldierin', then we kin buy all the goods ye got."

"No, you . . . you don't understand!" Amity stammered as she clung to him.

But he turned, flung open the door—and collided with Zeb Greene.

The innkeeper's son scowled. "Watch your step, woodrunner," he snapped.

Hannery looked down at Zeb. "Don't yarr at me, boy," he said, "or I'll have yer pa put ye on the spit for my dinner!"

Dave gave a snorting laugh. "Naw, don't do that, Hannery," he said. "Yer belly would rumble for a week from all the fat on this here goose." He jabbed Zeb Greene in the middle and laughed as the boy's shirt spilled out over his breeches.

"Quee down, you fellers," Tim Murphy said. "C'mon, I'm standin' grog fer the three of us." He pushed his friends out the door and steered them down the brick walk. Dismayed, Amity watched them head across the street toward the inn.

"Amity!" Polly said. "How unlike you! Whatever in the world—?"

Zeb Greene looked up from stuffing his shirt back into his breeches. "You again!" he said as he thrust his fleshy face close to Amity's. "Aye, the very one who was with the peddler last night. What are you about?"

"Hush, Zeb," Polly said. "Amity is my friend come to visit, and she's brought the best news about my br—oh!" She winced as Amity's foot came firmly down on her own.

No talk of Matt, Amity pleaded silently. From Zeb Greene to Cheppa John is but a tongue's length. Ignoring Polly's bewildered stare, she said quickly, "Well, Zeb, did you come to buy something?"

He flipped a coin onto the counter. "Pa sent me for some snuff," he said. "The peddler didn't bring any this trip."

But he brought you a pair of slavey dogs, Amity thought, and with that thought everything suddenly came clear. The dogs! If she baited Zeb carefully, he could be her key to the inn.

She forced herself to smile at him. "Are you pleased with your new pets?" she asked.

"Turnspit dogs ain't no pets," he snorted.

Amity put on a look of wonder. "Whatever in the world are turnspit dogs?" she asked.

Zeb puffed with importance. "Dogs that do kitchen work," he boasted.

"Dogs doing kitchen work?" Amity said. "I can't imagine such a thing. Can you, Polly?"

Polly only gawked at her.

"It's true," Zeb insisted. "They're hard at it right now, doing my job for me."

Amity shook her head. "No, it can't be," she said. "I can never believe such a thing unless I see it with my own eyes."

"Then come see for yourself," he burst out. "Then you won't doubt me."

She had done it! "Oh, I must see this strange thing!" she cried. "Polly, I'll tell you all about it!" Leaving Polly still staring wide-eyed, she ran for the door. "I'll not be long," she called back.

Just long enough to draw some riflemen aside in private talk. To slip them the buttons. To explain about the letter.

She had no idea how she would manage it, but once she was inside the inn something . . . something! . . . would come to mind.

The common room of the inn seemed wrapped in twilight. With its dark ceiling beams and smoke-filmed windows, it was a world apart from the sunlit day outside.

Amity stood in the doorway, willing her eyes to get used to the gloom. So much smoke, she thought. Greasy yellow as it rose from tallow candles on the walls, blue as it curled up out of tobacco pipes, it made her eyes smart and her throat sting. As she followed Zeb into the haze, she tried to take shallow breaths. It would not do to call attention to herself with coughing.

Voices swirled around her, deep rumbling voices gusting from groups of townsmen who sat at thick oak tables or stood near the tapster's counter at one side of the large room. Where are the riflemen? she wondered as she followed Zeb, who was pushing his way importantly through the crowded room. And Cheppa John? she thought with a sudden shiver. What if he is here too? She looked around carefully, and let out her breath in relief when she saw no sign of him.

A serving girl bustled past, her face red and moist, wisps of pale hair straggling from her cap. Dark, foamy ale sloshed from the pewter mugs she set down in front of two men. Amity thought one of them was the blacksmith, but in the smoky haze she could not be sure.

Suddenly she saw them—Hannery, Dave, and Tim Murphy. Talking and laughing, they were sprawled at a table in a corner near the hearth, their long rifles leaning against the wall. Amity shot a quick glance at Zeb. He was giving the packet of snuff to the tapster and paying her no mind. She could just slip over to . . . no, impossible. The innkeeper himself was heading toward the riflemen's table, smiling and nodding, rubbing his hands together.

Amity pressed against the wall. She watched as Thaddeus Greene put eggs, cream, molasses, rum, and beer into a large earthen bowl. He lifted a red-hot poker out of the hearthfire and plunged it into the bowl, stirring the bubbling liquid until the hissing stopped.

"Ah then," Thaddeus Greene said as he swirled a lump of butter into the bowl. He made a great show of pouring the foaming brew into mugs. "Nowhere in York Colony will you get finer flip than this," he said proudly.

Hannery took a deep drink. He set down his mug and wiped his mouth on his sleeve. "Aye, Master Greene, ye be right," he said. "'Tis worth settin' out there in the mud all this time just to come here and sample Blue Eagle flip."

The innkeeper smiled as he refilled the mugs. "Ah, such an annoying stalemate. Will it last much longer?" he asked smoothly. "Does our General Gates plan a move against Burgoyne?"

Hannery shrugged. "Granny Gates don't tell us nothin'," he said.

"Surely you must hear talk around camp," the innkeeper said with a casual air.

"Naw," Dave said. "Only thing we hear is hoot owls up in the trees. I tell ye, I ain't had a full night sleepin' since I came to this here river country. Right, Hannery?"

Hannery nodded. "And the durned things ain't even good to eat," he said. "Tough as a Tory's hide."

Amity watched the smile slide off Thaddeus Greene's face. He turned away to another table. Now, she thought. Just a few steps and . . .

"Aren't you coming?" It was Zeb, pulling her arm and scowling.

She bit her lip. "My eyes . . . the smoke . . . I lost track of you," she stammered.

"In here." He pushed her through a doorway into the inn's kitchen. "There! See for yourself!" he said, and pointed toward the stone hearth that took up a whole wall. "Isn't it wonderful?"

To Amity it was terrible. "Oh!" she gasped, and all thoughts of the riflemen fled.

Twig was harnessed to a platform of moving slats bolted between two upright iron wheels that clanked as they turned. It was his running that made the platform move and the wheels turn—fast, steady running that had him panting. The white fluff of fur on his chest was mashed flat by tight leather harness straps, and his white-tipped tail quivered. Horrified, Amity traced the motion of the wheels to rods that turned a long spit of geese sizzling over the fire.

Zeb took Amity's silence for admiration. "Pa made the smith put it together first thing this morning," he said. "But see this? I built it myself." He pointed proudly to a rough wooden cage, its slatted sides made of sticks crudely nailed together. In it lay Chip, his eyes closed, his head on his paws.

Suddenly Twig saw Amity. He broke stride, but the momentum of the wheel carried him on and tipped him over onto his side. Paws scrabbling in the air, he twisted in the harness and struggled to stand, but he was helpless against the movement of the wheel. His yelps roused Chip, who scrambled up in his cramped prison and began to bark too.

"Oh, Twig!" Amity cried, and lunged at the wheel. The metal bit into her hands, but she held on until it rattled to a halt.

"What the devil are you doing?" Zeb shouted angrily, but she paid him no mind. She knelt down, righted the little dog, and stroked him, feeling the swift thud of his heart. He licked her fingers and his tail whisked back and forth against the spokes of the wheel.

"You can't stop the spit—the geese will burn!" Zeb shouted.

"Bother your old geese!" Amity murmured under her breath, but she forced the anger out of her voice as she said, "Your dog may be hurt."

"He better not be!" Zeb cried. "Pa's like to thrash me! He paid gold for these little beasts!" As he clumsily unhitched the harness, Amity scooped Twig up in her arms and held him close.

Zeb frowned at the dog's paws. "Naw, he's sound enough," he decided. "Give him over. Got to get the birds moving again."

Amity drew back. "No," she said. "He's too tired to run anymore."

He gave her a sour look. "Well, one's as good as the other," he muttered, and lifted the crude latch on the wooden cage. He pulled Chip out, dumped him onto the treadmill, and harnessed him. "Run!" he ordered.

But Chip twisted around, snapping and growling, trying to bite Zeb. The boy's face darkened. He tonged a red ember out of the fire and dropped it between the dog's paws. "Run, curse you!" he shouted, then laughed. Chip, skittering away from the piece of hot wood, had set the treadmill in motion. "I thought up that trick myself," he said smugly.

Amity clamped her teeth over her anger. Cradling Twig, nuzzling him with her cheek, she wondered how to get out of this kitchen back to the common room and the riflemen.

It was not a pleasant kitchen. In the center stood a thick wooden table heaped with sausages and hams, half-gutted fish, chunks of onions, platters of gingerbread. The odors clashed sickeningly. A large basket of fish stood in a slimy puddle on the stone floor, and geese hanging from iron hooks were still feathered and crusted with blood.

"Ho, Zeb!" a voice said suddenly. It was the serving girl, carrying a tray of pewter plates that she set down with a clatter. "Your pa's been asking for you. Best get yourself out to help him afore he takes a fit."

She looked sharply at Amity, then softened when she saw

Twig in her arms. "Nice little dogs, ain't they?" she said. "Near scared out of their skins they've been, ever since the peddler brought 'em in last night."

"Where is the peddler now?" Amity asked.

The young woman shrugged. "Gone off somewheres. Oh, I do like this one." She cupped Twig's nose in her hand and made little crooning noises at him.

Zeb snatched the dog away. "Don't be going all softheaded over the dogs, Celia," he snapped as he thrust Twig into the wooden cage. "They have work to do, and so do you."

Celia gave Amity a wink. "Oh indeed, Master Zebulon," she said with mock respect. "Indeed, there's no lolling about for any of us today, now that Cook's gone."

"Gone to where?" Zeb asked as he cut himself a thick chunk of sausage.

"Took himself off to his bed, he did, holding his belly and groaning with the flux," Celia answered. She twitched her rumpled apron. "Left a pretty mess here, didn't he? These fish will spoil if they're not cooked up soon."

Zeb merely grunted. "Then do it," he said, and flung himself down on a bench, chewing with loud smacks as he watched Chip work the wheel.

Amity looked closely at Celia. Do I dare ask her help? she wondered. No one questions a serving girl being in the common room. I could give her the buttons to hide in her apron pocket, and she could pass them along to the riflemen, and . . .

But what if she's a Tory, like Zeb and his father? What if she's part of their family? Best find out more about her.

Zeb was sprawled on the bench, drinking great gulps of cider. She turned her back on him and moved close to Celia.

"What a fine place the Blue Eagle is," she said casually. "Have you . . . worked here long?"

"Too long," Celia muttered. "Only came to this town so's I could be closer to my husband, Bert."

So she's not family with the Greenes, Amity thought with relief. But she might be a Tory just the same. Is Bert the cook? Amity wondered. Not likely, the way Celia had spoken about him, not even giving him a name.

But Celia said nothing more. She slid one of the sizzling geese off the spit onto a wooden platter and laid it on the table.

Amity tried another question. "Is the inn always so busy?" she asked.

"Busier than usual these past days," Celia said. "Continentals, mostly. Guess they don't have much to do, with them armies just sittin' up there, neither one makin' a move."

Amity held her breath. "For a fact, though," Celia said in a low voice, after a quick glance at Zeb, "I like a sittin' war better than a fightin' one."

"Wh-what do you mean?" Amity asked.

Celia lowered her voice to a whisper. "Because of Bert," she said. "He's up there with the Patriot army."

She plunged a carving knife into the goose, and as the steam billowed up Amity's hopes rose high with it.

CHAPTER

18

❖

A shout from the common room lifted above the buzz of voices. "Ho, landlord, where's our food?"

Thaddeus Greene hurried into the kitchen, his innkeeper's smile turning to a scowl. "Why are things so slow?" he snapped at Celia. "Where is Cook?"

"Took with the flux," she answered, drawing the knife through the steaming goose. "You'll not see any more of him this day."

"The devil take him!" stormed the innkeeper. "Near midday and the inn filling—a fine mess he's left me in. Zeb, you lazy dolt, on your feet!"

He jerked the boy off the bench and cuffed him. Thrusting the platter of sliced goose at him, he ordered, "Take this out to the woodsmen in the far corner. Step lively, and mind you don't spill in anyone's lap."

Zeb thumped off, and Thaddeus Greene turned on Amity. "And who might you be?" he demanded.

Amity found her voice somewhere. "A . . . friend of Zeb's," she said. "Come to admire the dogs."

The innkeeper peered at her suspiciously. "Have I seen you

before?" he asked. "No matter, just keep yourself out of the way."

He turned back to Celia and ordered, "Stay here in the kitchen. Cook the fish and string more geese on the spit. And be quick about it, or no wages will you see from me this day."

He slid a ham onto a platter and made for the door. "Mind you keep the dogs going," he called back. "Don't let those birds burn."

Celia watched his broad back vanish into the common room. "Did you see him clout Zeb?" she said to Amity. "Time was I felt sorry for the lad, him being motherless and all, till I saw what a lazy, whining oaf he is. Likely he'll be bragging all over town about his turnspit lackeys."

Her face puckered as she glanced at Chip running on the treadmill. "Poor little creatures," she said. "Worked to death they'll be, while Zeb takes his ease and grows fatter. *Pffah!*" She yanked a goose down from the rack and began pulling out its feathers.

"Let me help," Amity said.

For a while they worked at the birds silently. Then Celia looked up. "What might be your name, child?" she asked.

Amity told her. "It's a word that means friendship," she added. "And peace."

Celia sighed. "We could do with both these days," she said.

"You said . . ." Amity ventured, "your husband is up at the camp, with our army."

"Aye," Celia said. "What about you? No marriage ring on your hand. Do you have a sweetheart?"

Cheppa John's face flashed before Amity. "I thought once . . . No, I don't have a sweetheart. But my father is fighting with the Patriots too."

Celia gave a nod of sympathy. "It's hard when someone close goes off a-soldiering," she said. "My Bert came out of Freeman's farm with nary a scratch, but oh, I fear the thought of another tangle with Burgoyne. Some say he's bound to try another attack, but nobody knows when."

Tomorrow! Amity cried in her head.

Thaddeus Greene bustled back into the kitchen. "Bread, quickly!" he snapped at Celia. "Haste, haste girl—the general will be here soon. Curse that cook and his ailing belly!"

He rushed out with a basket of loaves. "What general is he expecting?" Amity asked as if she were merely curious.

Celia's eyes flashed. "General Arnold—the only *real* general this army has," she said. "Haven't you heard? Old Granny Gates huddles himself behind a line of sentries thick as your mother's porridge, but not Arnold. I do admire that man. Lame or not, he'd chase Burgoyne all the way back to Canada if Gates would only let him."

Amity was certain about Celia now.

"Celia, there's something—" she began, but shouts and cheers from the common room cut off her words. She ran to the kitchen doorway and saw Continental officers and riflemen raising their mugs in loud greeting to two men who had entered the inn.

"That's Arnold himself," Celia said over Amity's shoulder, but Amity did not need to be told. There was no mistaking the man she had seen the night before—the hawklike nose, the gold buttons lighting the blue tunic, the limp.

She peered through the smoky haze of the common room at the burly man who towered above him. "Who is the other?" she asked.

"Dan'l Morgan," Celia said. "Did you ever see such a strapper?"

Indeed, in his creamy-white buckskins Morgan seemed a giant. On his head he wore not a coonskin cap like the other riflemen, but a round hat of black felt, one side of its brim pinned up with a green ribbon cockade. Indian beadwork on his belt shone bright red and blue, and a large piece of carved birchbark hung around his neck on a leather thong.

"What's that around his neck?" Amity whispered.

"It's a whistle—makes a noise like a turkey," Celia told her. "Uses it to signal his men."

Though Arnold barely came up to the shoulder of this giant woodsman, he moved into the room with such a proud air that he did not seem a small man. Even the limp, Amity decided, did not diminish him.

Thaddeus Greene hurried over, rubbing his hands together and bobbing short little bows.

"Welcome, gentlemen, welcome," he said with an oily smile. "I've kept a table in readiness for you."

He led the way to a table in a private corner, held out a chair for Arnold, and bowed him into it. "Your comfort, sir," he said with another dip of his head, and placed a brass candlestick on the table.

Arnold eased himself into the chair, favoring his left leg, and drew off his white gloves. Thaddeus Greene hovered over his guests with fawning care, lighting the candle, tonging an ember from the fire and placing it in the bowl of Morgan's pipe, nodding and smiling as he took their orders.

Celia turned away from the door and began to spoon drippings over the geese. "They'll be wanting one of these birds for sure," she said.

Amity steadied herself. Now was the time. "Celia," she said, "help me find a way to speak with General Arnold."

"With General Arnold!" Celia stared, then her face softened. "Ah, it's news of your father you're after, isn't it? Oh, Amity, many a time I've longed to ask for word of my Bert, but it can't be done. Master Greene would never permit it."

"I must speak with him," Amity insisted. "I must!" She felt her voice rise and her fists clench.

"Bless me, I don't see . . . why, whatever makes you tremble so?" Celia said in alarm.

Amity swallowed, then unlocked the words at last. "I must speak with him because I . . . I have a secret letter, with word of the attack. It's . . . signed by General Burgoyne!"

Celia's manner abruptly changed. She jabbed an elbow at Amity and scowled. "Move aside, girl," she said, her voice suddenly hard. "There's jumble enough in this kitchen without you in my way."

Amity's stomach rolled over. The secret was told, and to the wrong person after all.

"What's signed by General Burgoyne?" It was Zeb Greene. He

was holding an empty platter and he had been licking his greasy fingers, but now he stopped, his eyes narrow and suspicious.

Amity turned away, lost for anything to answer, but Celia loosed a stream of words. "Assigned to General Burgoyne?" she cried. "You'd best watch your words, miss!"

Turning to Zeb Greene, Celia tossed her head. "Fancy, Zeb!" she said, "this girl asked if the inn might be assigned to General Burgoyne as headquarters if he takes Stillwater. Why, your good father, as loyal a Patriot as ever there was, would never permit such a thing. Assigned to Burgoyne indeed!"

As she ranted on, Zeb set down the platter, threw them both a sour look, and clumped back to the common room.

"Wasn't that a tight one!" Celia said softly. "And didn't I almost gag at calling his Tory father a Patriot! Now, where is this letter? Give it to me and I'll slip it to the general under cover of serving him."

"It's in pieces," Amity said. "We must cut it off my dress and patch it together so he can read it."

"Celia, what goes on here?" said Thaddeus Greene as he burst into the kitchen. "Zeb tells me you and this girl are chattering about matters that—"

"There's no call to bend your tongue at me, Master Greene!" Celia blazed. "You've set me a task in this kitchen to break the back of an ox. Mind you, it wasn't for cookery I hired to this job, but now Cook's gone and I'm scrabbling about in here like a sparrow in a windstorm and this girl has been a help to me!"

She waved the basting spoon, and globs of waxy white fat spattered him.

"Baste the geese!" she ranted. "See to the bread! Cook the fish!" She scooped a fish out of the basket and waved it in his face. "Well, sir, do you want their heads chopped off or do you want 'em put in the pot the way they were took out of the river?"

The innkeeper backed away. "N . . . never mind the fish," he sputtered. "Just get a bird ready for the general's table. I'll send Zeb to fetch it." Then he was gone.

"Ha!" Celia said as she tossed the fish aside.

Amity found her voice. "You know he's a secret Tory!" she whispered.

"Aye, and it fairly choked me to see the new signboard he means to hang out if Burgoyne wins. He thinks it well hidden, but I saw it this morning in the stable."

She paused then, and gave Amity a look that went from the neck ruffle on the shift under her dress to the tops of her shoes. "Cut your dress?" she said.

Amity clasped one of the buttons and stumbled for words. "Just . . . just these."

Celia's look became a stare. "Take the *buttons* off?"

Amity reddened. How in heaven could she hold her bodice together if the buttons were gone altogether? She didn't fancy anyone, least of all Zeb Greene or his father, seeing her with her dress agape to the shift underneath. "Just . . . the covers," she stammered.

"Celia!" Zeb's shout came from the doorway. "Pa says you're to ready food for General Arnold!"

Celia plumped a sizzling goose onto a tray of plates and cutlery. "Here!" she said to Amity under her breath. "Take this bird to the general's table and do whatever you need do. And good luck go with you!"

Amity snatched up the tray and made for the door.

"Hold on here!" Zeb said with a scowl, and would have blocked her way but Celia clutched his arm and pulled him into the kitchen.

"Zeb, come quick!" she cried. "I've not had time to change the dogs and this one's lagging with tiredness and if the spit doesn't quicken, the geese are like to burn!"

Amity hurried into the crowded common room. As she threaded her way between the tables, noise and clamor whirled around her, but it seemed as if she were outside it all, hearing and seeing from a great distance. Thaddeus Greene, mixing flip for a group of Continental officers, looked up at her in surprise and frowned, but she hurried past to the table where Arnold and Morgan sat deep in talk.

Her hands shook as she set the tray on the table. It's the moment finally come, she thought, and here I stand with no notion of what to do next.

Arnold looked up. "Well, lass, that looks tasty," he said. "Have you brought a knife, or are we to pull the bird apart with our hands?"

A knife? She looked down at the tray. There it was, a bone-handled carving knife. Bless Celia!

No time now for neatly cut threads and the careful removing of cloth. She snatched up the knife and in four swift movements slashed the buttons off her dress.

Arnold half rose from his chair. "What—?"

"General Arnold, sir," Amity gulped. "Here is . . . you must . . . oh, sir!"

Swiftly she slit the cloth coverings, peeled back the wool, drew out the hidden squares of paper, spread them on the table.

"Please read this," she begged. "Please!"

The frown he gave her was frightening, but he settled back in his chair, pulled the candle close, and squinted at the tiny writing. ". . . *attack the Americans* . . ." he read. ". . . *full assault with artillery* . . . What does this mean?"

"It's a letter," Amity whispered. "From General Burgoyne!"

Morgan bent to the papers. "God's truth, the lass is right," he said. "Here's Gentleman Johnny's own name at the end, writ by his own hand!"

Arnold's eyes burned into Amity. "What have we here?" he said in a low voice. "A Patriot spy? So young and winsome? Quickly, girl—how did you come by this?"

Somehow she found words to tell of Matt and the courier. "It was hidden in the canteen, between the leather and the tin," she told them. "My mother and I found it, and we put it into these buttons."

"By thunder, you and your mother have done a clever thing," he said. "And a bolder lass I've never seen!"

He peered closely at the bits of paper. "It sounds as if . . . aye, 'tis true! Burgoyne plans to attack us!"

Morgan ground his fist into his palm. "When?" he growled.

"*The seventh day of October,*" Arnold read. "By God's teeth, that's tomorrow!"

The two men stared at each other.

"Give ear to what the scoundrel has written!" Arnold said in a low voice. "*The surprise and force of such an attack will overwhelm the rabble . . .* Hah! Take care, Gentleman Johnny—you'll find your surprise turned on yourself!"

His eyes flashed as he leaned toward Morgan. "Daniel, hear me well. Take your men back to camp and post them beyond the fortifications. Leave no bit of woods unmanned. Do it quickly, and continue the watch through the night. We must know where Burgoyne is placing his men and artillery."

Morgan nodded. "I'll have my boys in the trees afore sundown," he promised.

"Good. Send me word the minute the redcoats advance. And, Daniel—let no enemy scout see our own preparations."

"Won't nothing bigger than a rabbit get past my fellers," Morgan promised with a grin. Then, looking at Amity, his big face wrinkled. "Ah now, lass," he said, "what a ruin you've done to your dress."

Amity flushed. There were holes where the knife had slashed into the wool, dangling threads where once there had been buttons. She clutched her dress together where it gaped open over the shift beneath.

Morgan pulled the green cockade from his hat. "Here, take this," he said, holding it out to her. "Tomorrow I'll get me a fancier one from Gentleman Johnny himself!"

Amity met his smile with one of her own as she pushed the pin into the soft wool of her dress. Colonel Morgan's own ribbon!

Suddenly a thick hand clamped down on her arm. It was Thaddeus Greene. "What's afoot here?" he demanded. "What's all this private talk? 'Tis a meddling miss you are, and no right person to serve the general." He shook Amity roughly, but Arnold and Morgan were on their feet now.

"Have done, landlord," Arnold snapped as he wrenched the innkeeper away. "The lass has served us better than you know!"

Morgan swept the squares of paper under his hand, but the innkeeper's shrewd eyes had seen them. He looked from the litter of button molds and cloth to Amity's dress, and suspicion flared in his face.

Arnold shoved him aside. "Daniel, rally your men!" he cried. "By heaven, we have Burgoyne by the tail now!"

Eyes glittering, he strode across the room as swiftly as his limp would take him. "To horse, boys!" he shouted at startled Continental officers. "Back to camp! We have work to do!"

A high-pitched gobbling sound rose above the scraping of chairs. It was Morgan's birchbark whistle, its turkey call a rallying cry for the riflemen. Chairs overturned, pewter mugs and plates crashed to the floor as riflemen, hooting and waving coonskin caps, leaped up and rushed after Morgan. Continentals made for the door in a blur of blue jackets and flashing buttons. Amity flung herself out of the way near townsmen who pressed against the walls.

"Pa! What's happening?" shouted Zeb Greene, cowering gap-mouthed beside a cupboard.

"That girl! She had papers hidden on her—a secret message!" The innkeeper pawed the littered table. "Meddling girl!" he shouted. "Spy!"

He looked around wildly and caught sight of Amity. "There she is!"

He lunged at her, but she slipped under his arm and ran toward Celia, who stood wide-eyed in the kitchen doorway.

"Celia! Help!" she cried.

It was not Celia's hand that caught her, but the hand of a man behind her, fairly jerking her off her feet. She screamed and kicked, but the man held her firm.

"Hold her! She's a spy!" she heard Thaddeus Greene shout. Red with rage, the innkeeper pushed his way around upturned chairs and tables.

"This girl!" he panted. "She passed a message to Arnold! Had it hidden in the buttons of her dress! Quick—take my best horse and warn Burgoyne something's afoot. Hurry, peddler!"

CHAPTER
19

Cheppa John spun her around.

"*Amity!*" His voice was a hoarse shout.

He gripped her hard as if she might vanish in the smoke. "What in heaven's name are you doing here?"

Then his eyes darted over the ruined dress. "Morgan's cockade? God's truth, what has happened here?"

"She passed a secret message to Arnold!" Zeb Greene shouted. "I knew there was something wrong about her!"

"What message?" Cheppa John asked in bewilderment.

"Something writ on paper—I saw it!" Thaddeus Greene panted. "All in pieces, and Burgoyne's name on one—like the close of a letter!"

"Letter?" Cheppa John snapped. "What letter? Answer me, girl!"

Squirming under his grasp, Amity locked her mouth tight.

"Shake it out of her!" Zeb Greene cried. "Whup her!"

"No, take her to Burgoyne!" the innkeeper said. "You, miss . . ." He gave Amity an angry shove. "The British have ways to loosen a spy's tongue. Quick, peddler!"

From outside in the courtyard came the clatter of boots, the neighing of horses, and men's shouts. Above it all Amity heard the shrill gobble of Morgan's turkey whistle.

Cheppa John's eyes bored into her. "Amity, speak to me. How in God's world are you mixed into this?"

Amity lifted her chin. She could meet his eyes now that the letter was safe in General Arnold's hands. "It seems," she said, struggling for breath, "that the world is more upside down than you thought!"

She twisted away from him and ran. Stumbling through a litter of plates and tankards, she raced toward Celia.

"This way!" Celia cried, and pulled Amity into the kitchen. "Out the stableyard door!"

But Thaddeus Greene, fat as he was, was upon them both, and the room filled with his shouts and curses as he flung Celia aside and pinned Amity against the wall of the hearth. "I'll show you what we do with spies around here," he raged. "Come quick, peddler! Off to Burgoyne, and take her with you!"

"Celia—help me!" Amity screamed, but the innkeeper's shove had tumbled the serving girl into a pile of baskets. As she struggled to her feet, Celia collided with Cheppa John.

"Out of my way!" he shouted, and rushed toward the hearth.

Under the innkeeper's grasp Amity struggled and kicked. "No!" she screamed at Cheppa John as he ran toward her.

But he did not reach for her. With both hands he seized the innkeeper and threw him to the floor. "Amity! Are you hurt?" he cried. "If he has harmed you I'll have his head!"

Amity could only stare at him.

The innkeeper was on his feet again. In a rage he lunged at

Cheppa John, but the peddler thrust him away with a blow that sent him crashing into the wooden cage on the floor. With a yelp the dog inside scratched at the broken slats.

"Pa!" Zeb shouted from the doorway. "Don't let the dog get out!"

The innkeeper rolled onto his side and lunged at the cage. To Amity's amazement Cheppa John slid it out of his reach and wrenched apart the broken slats till the dog was free. Then he seized the turnspit wheel with both hands and brought it to a clanking stop. In a swift movement he pulled the dog out of the harness and set him on the floor.

Barking wildly, Chip and Twig streaked around the kitchen.

"My dogs!" Zeb cried.

"My gold!" Thaddeus Greene roared. He heaved himself up and went puffing toward Chip. A stack of pewter dishes clattered to the floor as the dog raced away, ears laid back, paws sliding on the stone floor. While Chip dashed around in circles, barking furiously, Twig skittered behind the large basket of fish.

Zeb made a dive at Twig. "I have this little devil!" he shouted. "*Aaaiiiiii!* Pa—he bit me!"

"Celia!" bellowed the innkeeper. "Give a hand with the dogs! Quick, you miserable wench!"

Celia didn't move. Cheppa John raced to the basket and pushed his shoulder against it. Over it went, spilling fish and slimy river weeds onto the floor. The innkeeper lost his footing and went down with a bellow. His flailing feet caught Zeb and sent him sprawling in the slithering mess. Curses and cries mixed with the dogs' shrill barks.

Amity pressed against the hearthstone, too stunned to move. What is Cheppa John doing? she wondered frantically. And why?

Suddenly, quick as he had caught her before, he had her in his grasp. "Out the door!" he shouted, and pulled her into the stable-yard. She cried out and tried to twist away, but he held her tightly and clamped a hand over her mouth.

"Hush, Amity," he said. "You have no need to fear me."

Oh, but I have, she thought.

She quieted, though, and slowly he took his hand away. "A letter from Burgoyne, was it?" he said. "However in the world would you come to such a thing? What was in the letter?"

His knowing could do no hurt now. "Burgoyne plans another battle," she said, lifting her chin defiantly. "But now our army knows when."

She could not read the look he gave her, or understand why he threw back his head in a sudden, short laugh. "Oh, Amity Spencer," he said, as if he savored her very name in his mouth. He drew her around the corner of the inn. "Come and see the brew you and your letter have set to boil."

She blinked in the sunlight and stared.

The innyard was swirling with men and horses. Roused by Morgan's piercing turkey blasts, riflemen and Continental officers had come dashing from all parts of the town. Harness brass glinted in the sun as horses pulled at their bits and reared.

Morgan himself was astride a gray horse, forming his men into a square. Amity saw Hannery and Dave jam their coon caps down on their heads and shout to Tim Murphy, who grinned and patted his long rifle. Everywhere she looked there was motion, noise, excitement—horses pawing the cobblestones, men shouting, riflemen falling into place before Morgan, townspeople milling about at the edges of the innyard. And in the midst of it all Arnold sat high on his big stallion, his eyes flashing.

A boiling brew indeed! Amity thought. Well, let Cheppa John and the innkeeper do their worst. It's too late now for Burgoyne to catch our army by surprise.

A shouted order from Arnold brought the men to silence. Amity saw that he had risen in his saddle, sword held high above his head. Now he waved the sword in a circle and slashed it down, snapping out an order to the Continentals. They spurred their horses and clattered past him out of the innyard, harnesses jingling, and Amity watched them gallop up the road in a whirl of dust.

Arnold swung his horse around to face Morgan. There was another wave of the sword, another command. Morgan blew a long blast on his turkey whistle, and the riflemen stepped off with long, swift strides. Rifles slanted against their shoulders, shot pouches and powder horns swung at their hips, and in a moment they too were out of the innyard. Morgan rode beside them, the fringe on his white buckskins fluttering and the birchbark turkey call bobbing on his broad chest.

Arnold sheathed his sword. With a nod to the Continental officer mounted beside him, he urged his horse forward. Then suddenly, as if he had forgotten something, he drew the animal up and wheeled him around.

Amity stared. "General Arnold is riding to us!"

He halted his horse in front of them. With a swift, graceful movement he swept off his hat and made Amity a bow. She clutched her skirts and managed a wobbly curtsy.

Arnold smiled. Over her head his eyes met Cheppa John's for a long moment. Then he leaned down in the saddle.

"You surprise me, Cheppa John," Arnold said in a low voice. "Searching the countryside to find Burgoyne's letter for me, only to have this girl serve it up with my midday meal!"

Both men laughed. Touching his spurs to his horse, Arnold whirled the animal around and rode off. Soon there was nothing left but a scud of dust drifting toward the Blue Eagle signboard.

Amity stood frozen, slowly patching together the pieces. Cheppa John refusing to turn her in to Burgoyne. Keeping the innkeeper from hurting her. Freeing the dogs and going against the innkeeper and Zeb in the kitchen.

Sharing that wry laughter with Arnold.

"Searching the countryside to find Burgoyne's letter for me," Arnold had said.

She turned slowly. Her eyes met his and saw no shadows in them. "You . . . you are a spy for *Arnold!* " she whispered.

The lift of his eyebrows, the nod, the smile told her it was so. "In truth," he answered. "I've been his informant ever since Burgoyne took up headquarters at Saratoga."

"But I don't . . . It cannot be!" she stammered.

"It can indeed, and it is," he said. "Think, Amity. A peddler can go where he pleases, and who is to question? It was easy to get into Burgoyne's camp, sell a few trinkets, and persuade Gentleman Johnny to use me as a go-between for his couriers' messages."

He gave a short chuckle. "Aye, these past weeks I've been one who fishes both sides of the river. Burgoyne thinks me his faithful message runner, and so I have been, but what he doesn't know is that first I ran his messages straight off to General Arnold!"

Amity stared at him, speechless. "But we thought . . . oh, Cheppa John!" she stammered. "I . . . I thought you were a spy for the enemy!"

His eyes darkened. "However would you come to such a thought?"

"Matt told us about . . . about seeing you in Burgoyne's camp. He said . . ."

He peered into her face. "Matt Thomas? What part does he have in this? For a fact, Amity, you have much to explain. How did you come to have Burgoyne's letter?"

Haltingly, she told him everything. ". . . and then, before he died, the courier told Matt to give the canteen to you. And when we found the letter hidden in it, we thought . . . none of us wanted to believe it, but Matt had seen you in Burgoyne's very headquarters, and . . . well, it seemed that you had gone over to the British. For money."

His glance locked into her own. "I will do much for gold, Amity," he said slowly, "but not betray my country."

In the silence she felt her face flame. At last he spoke again.

"Aye, that would explain much. You scarce looked my way all the way to Stillwater. Tight as a wagon spring you were, not like the girl I've known for so long."

There was a painful question that had to be asked. "Why did you let Matt's family go on thinking he'd been killed?" she burst out. "How could you be so cruel?"

His face clouded. "That was the hardest lie," he said, "and the thing that gives me the most regret. Last evening at the Widow Becker's I felt my tongue burn with the truth, but I dared not say a word. Try to understand, Amity. How could I have told them weeks ago that I saw Matt in Burgoyne's camp? Mistress Thomas's tongue, and Polly's, would have gabbled all over Stillwater. It would have ruined my usefulness to our army. And likely gotten me hanged as a spy by one side or the other."

He took her hand. "Do they know now that Matt is alive?" he asked. "You've told them?"

She nodded. "But they don't know about the letter," she said. "No one knows, except Mother and Matt . . . and you."

"And Arnold," he said with a smile. He peered at her ruined dress. "A clever hiding place, Amity. But I shudder to think of the danger you put yourself in. What a brave one you are."

Amity shook her head and looked away. "I'm not brave at all," she said. "I was afraid every moment. There's not a scrap of courage in me."

He grasped both her hands now. "Dearest Amity," he said gently, "do you take courage to mean lack of fear? No, my sweet, it's those who act in spite of fear who are truly brave. Like your father. Like Matt, going into the enemy camp. Like you."

The truth of what he said flooded over her. Being brave, she realized, has nothing to do with being unafraid.

She lifted her face and looked full into his eyes. There were no secrets hiding there now.

"Amity!" a voice cried. It was Polly, braids flying, eyes wide, shattering the quiet moment. "Whatever is happening? Where did all those soldiers go in such a rush? Oh, Amity, just look at your dress—whatever in the world!"

Now Celia was with them too, laughing. "Well, peddler, you made a grand show in our kitchen," she said. "And you, Amity—look how you've roused up the whole town!"

Now Amity saw that the courtyard swarmed with people. She caught sight of the blacksmith, the apothecary, and old Master Wells, who gestured excitedly with his cane. In a chattering group of women stood Mistress Fassett, out of breath, her lacy cap askew. Thaddeus Greene and Zeb were nowhere to be seen, but in the buzz of voices someone said the innkeeper's name.

"Cheppa John!" Celia said in sudden alarm. "What if Master Greene himself gets to Burgoyne? He'll warn him something's afoot with that letter."

"No matter now," Cheppa John replied. "There is no turning back for Gentleman Johnny. He will have had his men on battle alert these past days, and on the morrow he'll find our men waiting for him at every attack point."

"And General Arnold?" Amity asked. "Will Gran . . . I mean, will General Gates let him be in the battle?"

Cheppa John squeezed her hand. "You need not fret about Arnold," he said with a chuckle. "Where there's a fight he'll be in it, and not Granny Gates nor the devil himself will stop him."

"What *are* you all talking about?" Polly asked impatiently. "What letter? What battle? Cheppa John, why are you and Amity holding hands?"

Cheppa John drew Amity closer. "It seems, Polly, that your friend is not the quiet miss you used to know," he said. "She's near as bold as General Arnold himself and cunning as any trickster."

"You should have seen her!" Celia put in. "Slashing those buttons off her dress, fighting off Master Greene and Zeb . . ."

"I don't understand any of this," Polly said.

"No matter," Cheppa John said. "All you need know is that because of her, General Burgoyne will have a pretty surprise waiting for him tomorrow!"

He gave her hand another squeeze. "Amity, don't go far," he said. "I must see to something."

Amity's eyes followed him as he made his way through the crowd. She heard him whistling, and strained to hear. Yes, it was Burgoyne's tune again. What a delight to hear it this time!

She grabbed Polly and Celia and danced them around in a circle. She sang,

"If ponies rode men and if grass ate cows,
And cats should be chased into holes by the mouse,
If summer were spring and the other way 'round . . ."

She whirled them around faster, repeating the words, making up some of her own, until at last Polly and Celia begged to stop.

"Whatever are you doing, Amity?" Polly gasped. "I hardly know you!"

Celia tucked flyaway strands of hair under her cap. "It seems there is much to know in her," she said to Polly. "There are more pieces to your friend than either of us can imagine."

Polly stared. For once she was speechless.

CHAPTER

❖

Amity smiled at the baby in her mother's arms and tucked the quilt under his feet. Each crooked seam and uneven stitch showed in the sunlight, but none of that mattered now.

"This is an important day, Jonathan," she said. "When you are a grown man, you must tell your children you were here in Still-water the day Burgoyne surrendered."

Standing at the roadside with the others, in front of the Widow Becker's house, she felt the excitement that swirled all around.

So many people! It seemed as if the whole countryside had suddenly come to life and surged into the town. Since dayrise, carts and wagons had rumbled onto the river road, pulled by horses gone skittish in the jostling throngs. Children darted out of side streets to join the crowds, and riders on horseback strug-gled to rein in their mounts. Everyone was talking, shouting, calling out—and looking impatiently up the empty road to the north.

"I can't believe it's all really happening!" Polly said. The sun lit up her freckles and made her red braids shine like copper.

It was a crisp, bright morning after a week of rain and fog. For days after the battle, Burgoyne's overpowered troops had crept back toward their main camp at Saratoga through mud and mist. Day after day the Patriot forces had tightened a circle around them, then closed in. And now it was all over.

Amity bent to the baby. "Think of it, Jonathan—Father's safe, and coming back to us today!" she said. Cheppa John had gone to the Continental camp himself and had seen him, even brought a letter from him.

She peered up the road. How hard it was to wait.

"Why does it take so long to surrender?" Polly grumbled. "I wish they'd be quick about it."

Amity tried to remember what Cheppa John had told them—how the defeated enemy soldiers would march to a meadow outside their besieged camp, then stack their weapons, set down their cartridge boxes, and furl their flags. After that, Lieutenant General John Burgoyne, Commander of His Majesty's Expeditionary Army of the North, would step forward and sign the surrender agreement.

That grand, swirling signature! This time Gentleman Johnny would be putting its scrolls and flourishes on a paper declaring his defeat. Then he would hand his sword to General Gates and mount his horse. At the head of his troops for the last time, he would ride out of the meadow and lead his men through Stillwater. They would indeed have gained the river road, but as prisoners of war.

Amity felt her heart jump. She would see Burgoyne at last.

"Oh, no, Jonathan, you mustn't!" The baby's tug at the green cockade pinned to her shawl thrust Burgoyne out of her thoughts. She smiled at him and gently loosened his fingers. Morgan's gift was too precious to be a toy.

Matt, leaning on crutches, swung himself near. He was wearing his deerskin cap again. Though his mother had cleaned away the grime, it was scuffed and misshapen, but it sat on his red hair like a jaunty pennant.

How wondrous good that Matt was well again. And Jonathan too.

It had been days since Cheppa John had brought them to Stillwater—Matt and her mother and the baby. Even Ned and Lady and the hens. The sheep would have to do for themselves in the pasture. Their spiked wooden collars would keep them inside the fence, and if any were stolen or eaten by wolves, well . . .

"There are things more important now," Joanna Spencer had said firmly, and Mistress Thomas had agreed.

Aunt Kate had made room for them all, and days and nights of dosing and poulticing and physicking had followed. Now the nursing was over. Matt's leg still pained him, Amity knew, but his fever was gone, and baby Jonathan was smiling and rosy again. How wonderful to be standing here, ready to celebrate victory with them all.

All but Isaac Thomas. He had died with Matt's hand in his, and the sorrow of his death lay heavy on them all. It was the one thing that dimmed the bright promise of this day. Mistress Thomas, dressed in the black mourning shawl she had worn since her husband's death, reached out to touch Matt. Amity saw her do that often these days, as if to prove to herself that he was indeed alive.

Despair, then joy, then sorrow had been Nell Thomas's lot, all in the space of one autumn. Will she ever again be the way she used to be? Amity wondered. Will any of us?

Even Polly, under her usual brightness, would cloud over sometimes, as if she were thinking of her father. He had been claimed by disease, not by war, but he was as dead as if British guns had brought him down. Gone forever.

Her own dear father had escaped death in two battles. Soon he would come marching into Stillwater with the Patriot army, and the Spencers would be a complete family once more while the Thomases mourned. It was more than she could hope to understand.

She longed to share her feelings with Cheppa John, and scanned the crowds for him. Why isn't he here? she wondered anxiously.

She'd seen little of him these past days. It seemed as if he were all over the valley, and during his quick visits to Aunt Kate's they were never alone.

Amity sighed. It had been hard to dodge Polly's prying questions, and even harder to pretend she didn't see Matt's questioning looks whenever Cheppa John was near.

"Do you have another secret, Amity?" Matt had asked once, and she had flushed red. It was too soon. If she and Cheppa John were to make a pair, he must speak to Father first, and Father must give consent. Mother would have her say too.

What would their response be? Amity had wondered. What if they refused to let her share the life of a wandering peddler?

But Cheppa John might not wander forever. She had seen him eye Aunt Kate's shop with greater interest than usual. After a while we might settle down to be town folk, with a shop like Aunt Kate's, she thought. But different, for the shop would be well stocked with books. She could see the sign:

JOHN CHAPMAN

GOODS

BOOKS

"Oh, Mistress Chapman, read to us!" the town children would beg, and she would gather them around her in a special corner of the shop and read aloud of Robin Hood and other chapbook heroes.

Mother had taught her and Simon to read as soon as their small hands could hold a hornbook. Father had taught them to think and question and wonder. Surely parents like that could not refuse her a life with a man as knowing and thinking as Cheppa John.

But where was he? The day before, she knew, he had gone south on the river road to trade, but surely he would be back by now. Wherever could he be? And why didn't Father and the others come?

"Gracious, Amity, you've caught Polly's fidgets," Joanna Spencer said, but she said it with a smile. She seemed many years younger this day. The worry lines had faded and her face was lit with excitement.

A pair of small boys with sticks over their shoulders came strutting out of the crowd at the innyard across the street.

"Look at me—I'm Gentleman Johnny!" one of them shouted.

"No, I am!" the other cried. "You're not big enough!"

"I am too!" the first shouted, and kicked road dust at his friend. The scuffle went on until their mothers ran out of the throng and pulled the small Burgoynes apart by their ears. One of them squirmed out of his mother's grasp and threw a clod of dirt into the air. It struck the Blue Eagle Inn sign that swung over the heads of the crowd.

The cobbled innyard was swarming with people, but the inn was tightly shuttered. It had been closed since Burgoyne's defeat on October 7.

"I wonder where Master Greene and Zeb are," Amity said.

It was Aunt Kate who answered. "Run off to Canada one step ahead of the tarpots," she said.

And Chip and Twig too, no doubt. Zeb and his father must have caught them, Amity thought with a sigh. Before long Zeb would have them working a turnspit somewhere in Canada.

Polly peered impatiently up the road. "There's not a sight of anyone," she complained. "I wish they'd be quicker about surrendering."

Balancing on his crutches, Matt tweaked her braids and grinned. "Likely it's taking Gentleman Johnny a long while to choose an extra-fancy uniform for this day," he said.

"Oh, I wish we could be there to see it all," Polly cried. "I would so like to see Burgoyne hand over his sword. Don't you wish we were there, Amity?"

Amity shook her head. She was content to be here with Mother and the Thomases and Aunt Kate. Not far away stood Ben and Charity Tyler. Charity wore the blue dress she had been married in, its silver buttons flashing in the sun. Amity saw Ben's arm hang limp at his side and guessed his wound had done him lasting damage. His other arm, though, was around Charity's waist, and Amity felt a pang. She longed for Cheppa John to be here, standing close beside her.

Polly's pinch made her jump. "Here comes Mistress Fassett!" Polly hissed.

Mistress Fassett was elegantly turned out in a rose brocade gown trimmed with lace. Her small, sharp face peered out of the blue silk bonnet she had bought at Aunt Kate's shop, and she moved toward their little group with dainty steps.

"She's been telling everyone that of course she always knew Burgoyne would be defeated," Polly whispered. "Such a silly creature."

"Look!" shouted one of the small Burgoynes, who had run out of the crowd again.

A boy on horseback was galloping down the road waving his hat. "They're coming! They're coming!" he shouted.

There was a cheer from the crowd, then everything went quiet. In the stillness Amity heard the faraway whistle of fifes, then the rattle of drums, louder and stronger with each beat. She felt Polly touch her arm.

"Look!" Polly cried. "It's our own army!"

The Continentals marched in ranks that shifted unevenly, as if marching were an unmastered, unimportant skill. Some kept pace with the drums, others tried to match their steps to those ahead or next in line, but most just walked along, grinning and nodding at the crowds.

"They fight better than they march," Matt said. He took off his cap in salute, and Polly jumped up and down waving and cheering.

Except for the officers, the Patriot army did not look at all soldierly. The Regulars had no more uniform than white crossbelts over their jerkins and shirts. The guns they held at all angles were an odd assortment—old bell-mouthed flintlocks, a few short, thick fowling pieces, even an occasional ancient French blunderbuss. Only a few men had muskets with bayonets, and Amity saw a strange jumble of shot bags, powder horns, and cartridge boxes slung over their chests.

Mistress Fassett sucked in her breath. "Whoever would have thought it?" she said. "Burgoyne defeated by such a ragbag army!"

"In truth, they are a shabby lot," Aunt Kate replied, but her eyes shone with pride as she watched them pass.

"Here comes the Stillwater militia!" someone cried, and the cheers rose to a roar.

These men looked even more unsoldierly, but the cries of the townspeople straightened their shoulders and lifted their heads. Amity felt her mother tense. She pushed closer and searched the ranks anxiously, dark questions in her mind.

Where is Father? Why can't I see him? What if Cheppa John was wrong and he was wounded after all? What if he has fallen ill, or . . .

Oh, let it not be so! she cried silently as more men marched by.

"Look!" Polly cried. "The valley men!"

All of them were so bearded and shaggy that Amity hardly knew them, but now she could pick out Dorf the miller, with his arm bound up in a cloth, and Karl Vrooman, and big Farmer Nash, and Schoolmaster Jowdy, with a bloodstained bandage around his head.

But where was the one who mattered most?

"Compan-ee, halt!" someone ordered. The men broke ranks before the order to fall out, and suddenly she saw him.

"Father!"

Will Spencer was so thin that his clothes hung on him and his skin stretched tight over the bones of his face. But his eyes shone as he reached out hungrily to his wife and children.

Joanna Spencer wept as she and the baby disappeared into his arms, and Amity, clasped in his tight grip, let her own tears flow.

"You *are* safe!" she cried as she clung to him. "Oh, it's true, you *are* safe!"

All around there was shouting and cheering, even laughter, but to Amity the only thing real was the rough homespun of her father's shirt against her cheek.

Jonathan squirmed against the tight press of their embrace

and began to fuss, and at last Joanna Spencer pulled away. Her face was wet with tears, but the sun had come up in her eyes.

Amity clung to her father. "I have so much to tell you," she said.

"I know," he answered, smiling down at her. "I had part of it from Cheppa John—about Matt and Burgoyne's letter and how daring you were."

"Did he tell you about . . . anything else?"

"Aye, he told me of his hopes and plans for the future," Will Spencer said. "It seems they include you."

Amity held her breath.

"I told him . . . well, we must talk, your mother and I," he went on. "But I gave him my blessing, and I'm certain she will too."

Amity leaned into the circle of his arm and closed her eyes for a moment. It was everything she had wished for.

"Ho!" a voice cried, "here's our lad Matt!"

"Alive, I'll be bound!" said another. "Just as the peddler said!"

In the swirl of shouts and handclasps and backslaps, Amity turned at last to look at the men crowded around Matt.

How changed they are, she thought. How much thinner, and older. Karl Vrooman's round face had deep lines in it, and even Farmer Nash, with his wide shoulders and deep, hearty voice, seemed drawn and weary. Schoolmaster Jowdy's yellow coat was torn, and the duck feathers were gone from his battered hat.

"Why, Master Jowdy, you're wounded," Amity heard her mother say.

He touched his bandage and made light of it. "'Twas only a piece of cannon wadding hit me," he insisted, but the shadows in his eyes spoke of hard, heavy memories.

"Amity! Here's my Bert!" a voice cried. Celia, her face rosy with joy, pushed into the group, clinging to a tall young man in a tattered shirt and breeches.

"It'll take some doing to get him back to the way I sent him," Celia said happily. "But he's all of a piece, bless 'im, except where he got in the way of some grapeshot. We'll soon be off for home." She squeezed Amity's hand and said, "I can scarce wait to tell him what you did!"

"Tell him how much you helped," Amity said. "And don't forget to tell about Cheppa John and the dogs and the fish!"

Celia laughed. "As if I could forget any of it ever," she said. After a last hug for Amity, she steered Bert through the crowd, beaming up at him.

"Dogs? Fish?" Will Spencer said in a puzzled way. "This I haven't heard of."

Amity met her mother's amused glance and stumbled to explain. "Turnspit dogs," she said. "Two of them, working in the kitchen of the inn. Cheppa John freed them to make the innkeeper go after them instead of me, and—"

"Here come the riflemen!" someone shouted. She squeezed her father's arm. "Later," she promised, and spun around to look at Morgan's men.

They marched boldly, faces jubilant under their coon-tailed caps. Morgan paced his horse back and forth along their ranks, and Amity saw with delight that he had a golden cockade pinned to his hat. It stood arrow straight, glittering in the sun. She wondered if he had indeed taken it from Gentleman Johnny himself.

"Look there—it's Tim Murphy!" Farmer Nash shouted. "Him that swung the whole battle for us!"

Amity strained to see Murphy, glad he was safe. "What did he do?" she asked.

"Picked off General Fraser, Burgoyne's second-in-command, from high in a tree," Schoolmaster Jowdy said. "General Arnold spotted Fraser rallying the line for a new attack. 'Send up your best shot to get Fraser!' he shouted to Morgan—I heard his very words! And up Murphy climbed, and—"

"And shot Fraser right off his horse," Nash put in. "From two hundred yards away!"

"What a sight to see that line crumple!" Master Jowdy said. "Nary a redcoat had any fight left in him after that."

"What about the Germans?" Matt wanted to know.

Farmer Nash snorted. "Turned tail and ran with the rest," he said scornfully. "Not all the beatings from their officers could make 'em stay and fight."

Amity scarcely listened. Her throat had tightened at mention of Arnold. He should be here today, she thought. He should be parading past, sitting his horse proudly, bowing to the cheers.

He'd been the hero of the fight, Cheppa John had told her when he'd come with news of the battle. His daredevil spirit had fired the troops, even after the jealous General Gates had ordered him off the field. Ignoring the order, Arnold had led a furious charge, galloping on even after a German musket ball tore into his leg—the same left leg that had been lamed in battle before.

"He never stopped fighting," Cheppa John had said. "Not till another German bullet brought down his horse and it rolled over on top of him."

"Was . . . was he killed?" Amity had asked, hardly daring to breathe the question.

"Nay, he's alive," Cheppa John answered. "But he'll be no part of any victory march."

Indeed, a few days later Amity saw Arnold make his own journey down the river road to be doctored in Albany. He'd been propped up in an open wagon, his leg swathed in bandages and his face white with pain.

Wounded twice in the same leg, she had thought sadly. He'll be more lame than ever. "Do you think he'll ever soldier again?" she had asked Cheppa John.

Cheppa John's gray eyes darkened. "Not for Granny Gates," he answered in a tight voice. "Gates is claiming credit for the victory. Not a word about Arnold in his report to Congress."

"That's unfair!" Amity cried.

"Aye," Cheppa John agreed. "Glory for a general who doesn't deserve it, and no mind paid to a real hero."

Now Polly jogged Amity's elbow. "Amity, you're not watching! Stop wool-gathering and look!" she cried.

Led by a fifer and a drummer boy, a cluster of blue-uniformed officers on horseback had appeared. "Let's look for that handsome Captain Dunn!" Polly said.

Amity had no thought for Captain Dunn. She had seen, riding in the midst of the others, a stoop-shouldered man whose gray hair straggled over his collar. He wore the insignia of a general, but his dark blue coat was ill-fitting and plain. His nearsighted eyes blinked through thick spectacles, and his thin lips twitched nervously. There was something prim about him, like a fussy old woman.

General Gates! she realized with a start. Indeed he did look like one who would stay behind the lines fussing with maps and papers instead of soldiering on the battlefield like Arnold and Morgan. She hated this timid general for taking to himself the credit for routing Burgoyne's troops.

"Well, there's old Granny himself," said a mocking voice behind her.

"Cheppa John!" Amity whirled around. "You're here! I've been . . . oh!" She forgot the thin gray general, for Cheppa John was drawing a furry bundle out of the folds of his tunic.

"Twig!" she cried. She scooped the little dog into her arms, laughing as his white-tipped tail thumped against her and his tongue licked her face. "However did you—? Oh, Cheppa John!"

He grinned down at her. "Some folks downriver found him nosing around, looking hungry. Fed him up and kept him for company, but I claimed him for you."

"For me!"

"Aye," Cheppa John said. "He's lost his work at the inn. What's to become of him if you don't give him a home?"

Matt pushed close and patted Twig. "Amity told us about the dogs," he said to Cheppa John. "A pretty price he'll bring when you sell him again."

Cheppa John shook his head. "That I won't do," he said. "He is my gift to Amity."

Matt, seeing the smile that passed between Amity and Cheppa John, gave a small, sad nod, as if to himself, and turned away.

"No more turnspits for you now," Amity said to Twig. "You'll be a farm dog and run free!" In her mind she saw him racing about the pasture on his short legs, helping Ned go after the sheep. She gave him another hug. She loved Ned, but this little dog would be her own special dear for however long the farm was her home. And after that—well, he would go with her wherever the peddler's wagon took them.

"Amity spoke of two dogs," Will Spencer said. "Where's the other?"

"No one knows," Cheppa John said. "Not a hair of him was seen since they both bolted away from the inn the day of all the commotion."

Amity's father smiled. "A fine stir that must have been," he said.

"No finer anywhere," Cheppa John agreed with a chuckle. "There's some who won't forget it for a long time."

In Amity's mind she could see the innkeeper and Zeb rushing wildly after the dogs. "They didn't catch you after all," she said to Twig. "And now you're mine!"

She longed, even in the midst of all these people, to make a thank-you to Cheppa John that would tell him she knew the meaning of his gift. Once before, clasping the chapbook in her hand, she had held her feelings in check. Now it was even more proper that she hold back again.

But oh, to throw her arms around him! To thank him for this special, loving gift not only with words but with her heart.

There will be time later, she told herself. She looked into his eyes, hoping he would understand the secret in her words. "Do you remember the time you gave me the book?" she said.

"Aye," he said softly. "I remember it well." He reached to stroke the dog, and his fingers covered hers as they had that day.

"I do thank you entirely for Twig," she said, "and with all my—"

"Hush, everyone," said Mistress Fassett. "See what's coming now—a very rainbow!"

"It's Burgoyne's army!" Polly cried. "At last!"

CHAPTER

21

❖

The last militia company shuffled by like a bobbing wave of drab brown and gray. Far up the road a dazzling ribbon of red, blue, yellow, and green moved toward the town. The sun glinted on brightly polished breastplates, on buttons and buckles rubbed to a brilliant shine. As the glittering troops drew near, the cheers that had greeted the militia died away to an uneasy silence. People moved closer to each other, and mothers gathered their children tightly to them.

The enemy.

They have lost, Amity reminded herself. It's all over, and they have surrendered. But the old fear rose in her and she wanted to run from them.

Drummers came first, a mass of them, twirling their drumsticks and beating thunder. Twig quivered in Amity's arms and baby Jonathan screamed. Amity saw her mother cover his head with the quilt to shelter him from the noise. At last the drummers passed, but the throbbing beat echoed after them.

"Look!" Polly gasped as tall men in towering hats of black bearskin marched stiffly past. Short brass chains glittered across their chins, and silver epaulettes gleamed on the officers' shoulders.

"Grenadiers," Matt said. "Meant to scare the enemy with their size."

"They do scare *me*," Polly said in an awestruck tone.

A troop of officers on horseback clattered by, and Twig gave a lurch in Amity's arms. "Hush, Twig," she crooned, and nuzzled her face into his fur. "It's only horses. You needn't be—"

"Look up, Daughter," her father said in a low tone. "Here comes Gentleman Johnny himself."

General Burgoyne sat his horse as if he were a victorious hero.

"Isn't he handsome!" Polly breathed.

Indeed he was, and more than handsomely dressed. His red coat with its golden epaulettes and rows of gold buttons was faced with white satin and drawn back to display a gold-embroidered waistcoat. Lace ruffles frothed at his neck and cuffs, and rings flashed on his fingers. With his spotless white breeches, gleaming black boots fitted with golden spurs, and chestful of shining medals, he was more magnificent than she had ever imagined.

"Will you look at him with his head so high," she heard someone mutter. "He thinks he's parading before the king."

Amity thought of stoop-shouldered General Gates and of short, lame General Arnold. In looks they were no match for this elegant Englishman, and yet he was the beaten one and they the winners.

Holding Twig tightly, she strained for a better look. Burgoyne had large eyes and a strong jutting chin. His face seemed carefully blank under the gold-trimmed black hat that sat on a wig of white curls tumbling past his shoulders.

"This is not the way he planned his march down the river road," Cheppa John said in a low voice.

Amity nodded. Of them all, she thought, perhaps Burgoyne was the one whose world had gone most upside down.

There were no taunts or jeers from the crowd at the roadside, only silence that deepened as Burgoyne rode closer. But it was not a fearful silence now. It seemed to Amity that by their very stillness people were showing him their dignity and their strength. Suddenly a flash of rose and blue caught her eye, and she turned to see Mistress Fassett step out of the crowd. She was holding her skirts delicately at each side as if she were about to curtsy.

"Oh, no!" Polly gasped. "What can she be up to?"

Burgoyne reined in his horse, ready to receive a lady's tribute. But Mistress Fassett had no curtsy for him. She looked up into his face and there was scorn in her voice.

"Once you called us a rabble in arms," she said. "Well, sir, go back to your king and tell him that not even his finest army could master such a rabble."

Then, lifting her skirts above the dust of the road, she turned her back on him and walked away.

"Amelia! How bold of you!" Amity heard Aunt Kate say. Mistress Fassett made a show of patting the folds of her gown.

She said nothing, but Amity saw that under the blue bonnet her mouth was pursed in a small, proud smile.

This is indeed a day of surprises, Amity thought. She turned for another look at Burgoyne, but his scarlet-and-gold glory had passed by. Now it was the rank and file of his army that came into view.

Like their general, the British soldiers had determined to look their best. They had polished their brasses, oiled their boots, and whitened their breeches with pipe clay, but as they drew nearer, Amity saw how ragged and shabby they really were. Most of the red coats had been shortened to jackets, for cloth from the tails had been used as patches. The blue coats of the artillerymen were stained with black powder smudges and in some places were torn beyond mending. Amity saw split elbows and gaping seams, greasy stains that seeped through clay-daubed breeches, boots bound up with rags.

Up close the king's army was nothing but row upon row of gaunt, grim-faced men. They had no guns, no bayonets, no swords, no flags—nothing but the scraggy uniforms that hung from their thin bodies.

As Amity saw the hunger and humiliation on their faces, she felt a tiny jab of pity. "Why, they're a more ragged army than our own," she said softly. "I feel sorry for them."

"Sorry for the enemy?" Polly bristled. "Not I! They're hateful!"

Amity said nothing. She was watching a large group of

women shuffle pass, and again her heart felt heavy. Tattered and muddy, they looked as if they had been in battle too. Some of them pulled carts little bigger than barrows, filled with rags and kettles. All of them trudged along with shoulders bent and hair hanging down in their faces.

"The poor creatures," she heard her mother murmur.

These dull-eyed, dispirited women reminded Amity of Sal and the others in the group that had stolen Jess. Which are the more pitiable? she wondered—women like Sal whom war had chased from their homes? Or ones like these, who had left home willingly to go warring across an ocean?

After the British soldiers and their women had passed, the German troops came into view. Drummers in yellow jackets and pale-blue knee breeches led them, but their beat was slow and listless, and the men shuffled behind them.

Most of them are no older than Matt, Amity suddenly realized.

"So these are the ferocious German mercenaries," she heard her mother say quietly. "How young they look, and how frightened."

"Their officers have told them we Americans eat our prisoners," Cheppa John said.

Amity and Polly gasped. "Why would they say such a thing?" Amity asked.

"To make the men fight hard," he answered.

"But I thought every soldier fought hard," Polly said.

"Regulars do, for they are soldiers by choice," he told her. "But most of these lads didn't join up of their own will. They were grabbed out of their fields and sent off to troopships in chains. Sold to King George like so many head of sheep."

Amity drew in her breath. So they were not really soldiers at all, just ordinary farm boys, like Matt.

Still, she reminded herself, it was one thing to pity women who cooked and washed for their menfolk, then had to search battlefields looking for their bodies. These young soldiers had themselves borne arms. It had been German bayonets and cannon that had forced the Patriots to retreat from the battle in the cornfield. A German musket ball had struck Arnold, and another had brought his horse down on top of him. And hadn't Germans as well as British left farms in ruins and people lying dead all the way from Canada? It would not do to feel sorry for them.

Amity saw Matt shift on his crutches as German grenadiers passed—tall, broad-shouldered men with high, brass-fronted helmets that made them look like giants. Down each man's back hung a thick blond braid plastered with tallow, and grease-coated mustachios curled down past their chins. The reek of the tallow made Amity want to cover her nose. Twig squirmed in her arms, unsettled by the smell.

"See, Amity," Matt said, "it's just as I told you. They take fine pride in that hair of theirs."

Amity saw no pride at all. These slow-footed men looked shamed and beaten. In spite of herself she flinched to see officers jab gold-headed canes at stragglers and herd them back into line. She could not understand the language in which they shouted at the men, but their voices held ugly meaning.

Suddenly Twig almost leaped out of her grasp. "Hush, Twig, what is it? Oh! Whatever in the world—?"

Soldiers dressed in all manner of ragged, makeshift clothing had come walking slowly along with an odd assortment of animals. Some of the men had raccoons and foxes in their arms. Others carried cages made of sticks, in which there huddled wild ducks, quails, and pheasants. One young soldier cradled a woodland hare in his arms, stroking its fur as he walked. There were larger animals too—thin, nervous deer on leather leashes, and half-grown bear cubs that waddled along, tangling their chains as they nosed from side to side.

"Cheppa John!" Amity said. "Did they bring these animals all the way from Germany?"

He shook his head. "Caught them in the wilderness," he answered. "Tamed them into pets."

"But why?"

"Needed something to keep from dying of homesickness, I warrant," he said.

"It can't have been easy to find food for these animals," Joanna Spencer said.

"Or to keep others from eating them," Polly put in. "Imagine making pets of deer and rabbits!"

Amity held Twig tight. Her thoughts were in a muddle as she stared at the sad, shuffling group. Farm boys forced into soldiering far from home, needing comfort so much that they had resorted to taming wild creatures. Did they share their own rations with these animals? she wondered. Fight off other soldiers to keep their pets safe?

It's all so puzzling, she thought. Yet, she reminded herself, Simon would have done the same.

A sudden commotion tore her out of her thoughts. The hare had jumped out of the soldier's arms and leaped to the ground.

"*Ach, nein, Fritzle!*" wailed the soldier, a boy in rough ticking breeches and a torn jacket. "*Komm hier!*"

He lunged for it, but the hare scurried off into the crowd on the opposite side of the road. As the boy dashed after it, the other soldiers straggled to a stop.

Amity saw an officer raise his cane and run after the boy. "Halt!" he roared. "*Zurück gehen! Go back!*"

Townspeople scattered as the hare streaked past them and headed for the trees behind the inn. Amity held her breath. Oh, let him catch his pet! she prayed.

But it was he who was caught. The officer grabbed him by the jacket, yanked him around, and beat him fiercely on the head and shoulders. As the hare vanished into the trees, the officer forced the boy back into line, prodding him viciously.

"*Zurück! Zurück!*" he shouted. "Back! Back!"

Shocked silence settled over the crowd. Then there were jeers and angry muttering, and a few of the townsmen shook their fists at the officer. He paid them no mind. Striding up and down between the rows of soldiers, he struck at the men with his cane to bring them to order.

Amity watched the young soldier take his place in line. His shoulders slumped and his eyes were cast down. Blood trickled from his nose and ugly red marks had risen on his neck and face. He looked as if he were trying to hold back tears, and Amity felt her own eyes sting. When the officer raised his cane and shouted a command to march, she made up her mind.

"Wait!" she cried, and darted into the street. Dodging the startled officer and the shuffling men, she rushed up to the young soldier.

"Here!" she cried as she thrust Twig at him. "I give him to you!"

The boy drew back in surprise. Amity pointed at Twig, then jabbed her finger at the boy. "He's for you," she said.

He struggled to understand. *"Für mich?"* he said.

"Yes," she said, and pushed Twig into his arms. "Take him!"

The young soldier clasped the dog to his chest. Tears welled in his eyes as Twig settled in his arms and began to lick his face. *"Danke, Fräulein, danke,"* the boy murmured, and a smile crept across his swollen face.

Amity turned and ran back, not daring to think of what she had done.

Her mother's face was pale with shock, and Polly stood open-mouthed. Everyone was staring at her, but she dared not look at any of them, especially Cheppa John. Instead, she peered after the German unit. The soldier, holding Twig close and patting him, turned back to smile at her. *"Danke! Danke!"* he called.

Amity tried to smile back at him. Oh, Twig, she cried silently, gulping down tears.

Master Jowdy spoke softly. "It was 'thank you' he was saying, Amity. *'Danke'* is German for 'thank you.'"

"Amity!" Polly cried. "Your own dog! How could you do such a thing!"

She made herself turn toward Cheppa John, but could not meet his eyes. "I gave away your gift," she said. "To an enemy. I didn't mean . . ."

He put a hand under her chin and tilted her face to his. "It was right," he said gently. "There is a time to put aside hate."

Then she was in her father's arms. "Amity," she heard him say. "Oh, my dear, you do such honor to your name."

Suddenly she felt weary. She was glad when the last of the troops straggled out of sight and the last drumbeats died away.

Polly sighed. "It was not a rainbow after all," she said.

"No, it was more a patchquilt," Amity said slowly. "And so was our army," she added. She thought of the uniformed officers, the backwoodsmen, the Regulars with their ill-assorted weapons, the militia, the shopkeepers and schoolmasters and farmers, the men like her father and the almost-men like Matt. "A patchquilt," she said again. "Many different pieces stitched together."

"A fitting image for our new nation," her father said.

"Aye," Cheppa John agreed. "Pieced together of many parts but, taken all together, whole and strong."

Like people, Amity thought. She glanced at Polly, at Mistress Thomas, at Mistress Fassett, at her own mother and father. No one is cloth come off the loom in one piece, she realized. We're patchwork, every one of us.

A feeling of peace washed over her. The war was far from

over, but the impossible had happened—the Patriots had defeated Burgoyne's huge invasion force. Surely people who could do that could win a war.

A chill wind blew off the river. Amity drew her shawl closer, and felt Cheppa John's arm go around her. The warmth of him drove out the last scrap of the cold fear that had come with summer. Whatever the future brings, she thought, we'll meet it together, with trust come back and secrets put aside at last.

A NOTE FROM
THE AUTHOR

What a strange war the American Revolution was. Poorly trained, ill-equipped "citizen soldiers" fought against the best army in the world, and won.

It didn't begin that way. Again and again, after the American colonists boldly declared their independence from England, General George Washington's Continental Army crept away from British troops in defeat. By 1777, the time of this story, almost every battle and skirmish had turned into disaster for the colonists.

Meanwhile, across the ocean, France looked on, yearning for the defeat of its long-time enemy England, but refusing to join the fight.

"Send us ships and troops and supplies," the Americans begged the French king. "Help us win the war."

"Show us you can win a battle," the king and his advisers replied. "So far we have seen only bumbling."

So France did nothing, and the Continental Army bumbled on.

Then, astonishingly, the massive British drive to capture the Hudson River failed. When General Burgoyne's army was forced to surrender near the small village of Saratoga, New York, the Americans knew that this time they had not bumbled.

The king of France agreed, and soon French help was on the way, making victory certain for the new United States of America.

Lieutenant General John Burgoyne had seemed the perfect officer to overpower the rebellious colonists. He was dashing, daring, and clever, praised for his poems, songs, and plays, and he was in the midst of a brilliant army career, having helped the British capture Boston early in the war. A clever strategist and a skillful leader, he had persuaded King George that an invasion from the north would end the war. He looked forward to leading the invasion and returning to London as a hero.

He knew there would be problems. Moving south from Canada, his men would have to hack their way through miles of dense forest, drag cannons and supply wagons through swamps, build bridges over streams, navigate down rivers and lakes. But Burgoyne was certain that his mighty army could do it. It was a well-trained, well-supplied force of nearly eight thousand men, with a line of march nearly three miles long. There was a massive amount of artillery, all the way from small field cannons to huge twenty-four pounders, and hundreds of horses to pull them along. Over four hundred wagons carried gunpowder, ammunition, and food.

An additional thirty wagons were packed with items for the general's own comfort. For although the way lay through wilderness, Gentleman Johnny saw no reason to do without the luxuries he enjoyed. Even in the forest he planned to live elegantly, inviting his staff officers and their wives to dinners at which his butler would serve food prepared by his excellent

French chef. Company musicians would provide entertainment, and perhaps there would even be dancing.

Many officers took their wives along, for this was to be a glorious adventure. Hundreds of other women went with the army—cooks, laundresses, and seamstresses, who saw to the needs of the ordinary soldiers. There were manservants for the officers, farriers to look after the horses, and wheelwrights to keep the wagons in repair. The king had given Gentleman Johnny everything he would need for a smooth and successful military operation.

Burgoyne expected little danger from the Continental Army, since General Washington's troops were far to the south, trying to recover from their terrible winter at Valley Forge. Even if Washington were to send some of his ill-equipped units against the invasion, such a ragtag force could easily be scattered to the winds. "The Americans are but a rabble in arms," Burgoyne was fond of saying.

His strategy was clear. Once out of the wilderness, he would cross his army to the west bank of the Hudson River, set up field headquarters at a village called Saratoga, and give the men and horses a few days rest. Then on through farms and woodland to capture the small town of Stillwater, which would yield a prize—a road leading directly south along the river. Not a wilderness trail, but a real, packed-dirt road on which he would march his grand, glittering army all the way to Albany. There, as planned, he would be joined by a large force that had come along the Mohawk River from the west, and by General Howe, who would have brought his own fine army up from New York

Town. The northern colonies would be sliced away from the others, the war would be over, and the quarrelsome Americans would be forced back under the fist of England.

How the world would praise Gentleman Johnny Burgoyne then! His plan was perfect, and it could not fail.

But it did. And months later, when Lieutenant General John Burgoyne returned to London, it was not as a hero but as a prisoner of war on parole. The people who had been proud of their Gentleman Johnny gave him a new, scornful nickname. From that time on he was known as "The Man Who Lost America." For then, as now, it was clear that the British defeat at Saratoga was the turning point of the war.

The story told in this book is part fact, part fiction. General Burgoyne and his invading army, of course, were real. So were General Horatio Gates, General Benedict Arnold, and Colonel Daniel Morgan. All of them really were in that place, at that time.

Tim Murphy, the rifleman whom Amity met in Aunt Kate's shop, was one of Colonel Morgan's top marksmen. He used a double-barreled rifle that was unique for its time, and he rarely missed his target. According to accounts written by soldiers who fought in the battle, the British line crumbled when Murphy shot down General Fraser, one of Burgoyne's best officers. That one shot, historians say, may have turned the whole battle.

The rest of the characters—Amity Spencer and her parents, neighbors, and friends, Cheppa John the peddler, Captain Dunn, Captain Fitch, the people in the town of Stillwater—live only in this story. Their experiences and adventures came from my own imaginings.

Burgoyne's letter was made up for the story. However, he did send letters at various points in his campaign to General Howe and other colleagues-in-arms, begging them to honor his strategy and come to his army's aid. You can see some of the letters between the British generals, many written in code, at the museum near the battlefield at the Saratoga National Historical Park.

Most historians say that Burgoyne really did write "The World Turned Upside Down." The tune was so popular in England that it was played and sung in elegant drawing rooms as well as on the city streets. Strangely enough, in 1781, when at last England lost the war and signed a final surrender at Yorktown, Virginia, a regimental band played this very tune as the British soldiers were marched away in defeat.

Many of the German soldiers did have wild animal pets. Unlike their officers and the elite Regulars, the German foot soldiers were miserable in Burgoyne's army. Against their will they had been taken thousands of miles from home to fight in a war they knew nothing about, and they were homesick for their farms and villages. Some of the people who actually saw Burgoyne's defeated army march through Stillwater wrote descriptions of these young men and the animals they had caught and tamed.

Most of the enemy troops were held as prisoners until the war ended. When they were finally released, many British and German soldiers chose to stay in America. They settled in towns and on farms, married American women, and brought up their children as citizens of the country they had once fought against.

General Benedict Arnold was perhaps the one whose life was most changed by the Saratoga campaign. He recovered from the wound in his leg but not from the insult to his spirit at the hands of General Gates and the Continental Congress. Although Burgoyne paid Arnold a courteous visit in Albany and praised his heroism, Gates ignored him. So did the Congress, which refused him promotion and back pay even though it granted such things to men less deserving. Furious that twice he had nearly lost his leg in the service of a country that would not honor his brave deeds, Arnold became brooding and bitter. Three years later he turned traitor.

As commander of West Point, America's fortress on the Hudson, he plotted to hand over the plans of the fort to the British. The plot was discovered, but Arnold escaped. Eventually he joined British troops fighting against the Patriots in Virginia and was made an officer, but instead of being admired by his new comrades-in-arms, he was looked down upon and treated with scorn. Even in England, where he spent the rest of his life after the war, people shunned him as a man who had betrayed his own country. As he lay dying in London, he asked to be dressed in the old American uniform in which he had fought as a Patriot. "God forgive me for ever putting on any other," he said.

America never forgave Benedict Arnold's act of treason. At the Saratoga battlefield you will find no statue marking his heroic part in the battle. Instead, close to the spot where he was finally brought down, you will see, without any mention of Arnold's name, only a stone carving of an empty left boot.

Yes, it was a strange war, and strangest of all were the events that swirled around the upper Hudson River valley in the summer and autumn of 1777 and came to a climax at Saratoga. During those desperate days there may indeed have been young people like Amity, whose quiet lives were turned upside down as they reached deep inside themselves for courage they didn't know they had.